# Bones of Mine

# Bones of Mine

**L.W. Edwards**

First Edition
First Printing 2013
L.W. Edwards
*Bones of Mine*

Summary: Mystery novel featuring Addie Conroy private security professional.
ISBN: 978-0-9860562-0-8

Book format by alamacque publishing
Cover design by alamacque publishing
Author Photo by Jennifer M. Tjernagel - Studio 241 Photography

Black Onyx Press
721 Brook Lane
Shakopee, MN 55379
www.blackonyxpress.com

Printed in the United States of America

# CHAPTER 1

*Nowhere to go; nowhere to be.* Addie Conroy couldn't believe that she had a Saturday all to herself. Then again, it was her 30th birthday, which had to count for something. She leaned back in the old rocking chair, bathing in the warm sun that was streaming in through the screens of her gazebo. As she drifted off, she felt her breathing slow.

Suddenly, her body tensed; she was somewhere dark. Wolff and Marie were there. Addie could see a shadow coming around the corner. Who was it? She couldn't see his face, but she knew that figure. She tried to scream, but nothing came out. She tried to move forward and realized that she was on the ground. Where am I? Her face and hands were covered in blood. In the distance, she heard Marie scream. Addie lurched awake. Before she had even realized where she was, she found herself standing in a ready position. Every muscle tense, sweat was running down her face and a gun was in her hand pointing at the gazebo door.

Would the dreams ever end? It had been two years since that job. She relaxed and returned her gun to its place behind her back. Wow, the big 30, a weekend off, and she couldn't even enjoy an afternoon nap in the sun? She knew the reason for the dreams. Her Executive Manager of Operations, Holly, had reminded her a few days earlier that they needed to document the case files from the New Orleans job. Yesterday, Addie had thought about it all the way home. Holly was right they needed to close out the file. The only problem was that she still didn't believe half of what had happened in New Orleans or know why.

Six years ago, if anyone would have told her that she would leave her career in the Navy (after only 5 years) to get married and join her retiring commanding officer in his private security firm, she would've called them crazy. Now she wondered how she had ever lived without her husband. Even though he was five years her senior, she couldn't resist watching him while he worked. He had been working on installing new steps which would lead down to the walking trails below their house. He'd been working on this job for the past couple of weeks. She still couldn't believe how much she loved him. He was shirtless, his muscles wet with sweat as he drove a hammer down into a newly added step. She would offer to scrub his back in the shower when he was ready to go in, or maybe…

They met after she had accepted the job with Solomon. The company was supposedly named for King Solomon's secrets. Her commander wanted the firm to be regarded in the same powerful, limitless, and sought after way.

The goal of the three Senior Partners, all retired military officers, was to hire the very best. They wanted to accomplish what they were never allowed to during their military careers. In essence, they wanted to win without political interruption, and with every loop closed. Their main headquarters was located in Minneapolis, and their satellite operations in New Orleans and Panama.

The firm had made Addie an offer that she couldn't refuse, tempting her with a junior partnership and a luxury onsite apartment in Minneapolis. She would have the freedom to pick her own team, and a budget big enough to buy any 'toy' that would be needed to get the job done. The day she joined the firm, the partners told her that her apartment would not be ready for another month or two, which gave her time to take the advanced training as they referred to it, before starting her first assignment. A week after she finished the physical phase of her training, she was flown to Knoxville Tennessee. A limousine was there waiting to take her to a secluded plantation near Sweetwater. It was there that she endured four weeks of what they called 'brain training'. Their goal was to identify her predominate skills in perception, out of body projection, and many other things paranormal. Not only were they able to identify her talents, they assisted her in fine-tuning skills which changed her life.

When she returned from her first very successful assignment, she had expected to move into her new apartment. Her partners, however, put her up in a hotel until she had been briefed on the finer amenities of her new home. She called the contractor and set up a face-to-face meeting. She wanted to know everything about the construction, security, and of course if the concealed weapons room was made to her satisfaction. As soon as he walked into her apartment carrying his toolbox, something inside her clicked. Apparently, it clicked for him too. She soon learned his workmanship was as exceptional as the man. After a whirlwind courtship, much to the dismay of her partners, she and Martin married. Even though Addie did not use the apartment for more than three months, it would be well utilized for many of their clients and projects.

Shortly before they met, Martin had purchased a five-bedroom Victorian home in a secluded neighborhood along the Minnesota River. He'd planned to restore the home and sell it for a profit. He hadn't counted on falling in love with Addie, and her falling in love with the house. She found working on the old house and its gardens a welcome escape from her work. That is until her work found its way to the house next door.

# CHAPTER 2

"Addie, are you awake up there?" Martin called from below.

"Yes, I was just sitting here thinking about how much I love you, and the gazebo you built me," Addie answered, standing and waving down at him from the gazebo.

"Well wife, your quiet time is about to come to an end. Looks like the second most important man in your life is coming to read to you."

"Second man in my…?" Addie questioned.

Before she could say any more, their young neighbor Nick blasted through the gazebo door. He plopped down in the rocker opposite her, right on time for their daily reading session.

"Hey Addie, here I am. Did you notice that I'm on time today? I even remembered my book." Nick said, as he started slowly rocking.

"I see that Nick. What are we reading today?" Addie asked.

"I checked out a new ghost book from the school library. How does this sound? 'Gory Mischief, Legends of the Ghosts that Terrorize the Houses of 5th Street.' Want me to read it?"

"Sounds good and scary to me Nick," Addie answered, shifting in her chair to reposition her gun that was poking her in the back.

"Are you sure it won't creep you out?" Nick asked, sliding back in the wooden rocker and spreading the big book out on his lap.

"Nope, I can't say that it will."

"You know Addie, that's one thing I like about you. You're just like the rest of us guys." Nick said, beaming at her.

"Hey, speak for yourself kid. I don't think my wife is like any guy." Martin Conroy's voice bellowed up from below. He drove another board into the ground to begin forming the front to the next step. Last year, he decided to take a year off from his construction business to work on the house and yard. He built a gazebo for Addie, which faced the edge of the embankment behind their house.

If she wasn't away on assignment, in the evenings while Martin worked on the yard, Addie would come out to the gazebo area to keep him company. She practiced her Tae-Kwon-Do patterns and worked on one of the smaller flowerbeds around the property. Three times a week, she had an appointment with the neighbor boy, Nick. Whenever he dropped by, she would listen to him read to her, or she would discuss other subjects of interest with him.

At eleven years old, Nick was what they called an accelerated student at Riverside Middle School. The problem was there just weren't enough schoolteachers or teacher's aides to go around. When Nick told his literature teacher about his new neighbors, she and Nick's mother paid Addie a visit.

They wanted to know if Addie would have time to work with Nick on the side. They would provide the materials if Addie could provide the time. When the weather was good Martin and Addie's screened in gazebo, complete with rocking chairs and never ending chocolate chip cookies, provided him with the perfect study spot.

Nick jumped up off the rocker and walked to the back of the gazebo. He leaned his arms on the wooden frame and looked over the edge, down at Martin.

"You know what I mean, Martin. I mean, she doesn't wrinkle up her nose and look like a prune. She don't make those screechy sounds like that cat I threw the rock at last week, or the girls in my class when they hear the word bugger. And when I talk about creepy things, she already knows about most of them. She knows about a lot of neat gross stuff. Not to mention she carries a gun. She sure beats the girls my age. Where did you find her anyway?"

"I didn't, my mom did," Martin said, sitting down on the step he just finished and wiping the sweat from his forehead. "My mom use to do my bids. She bid on a construction job at Addie's office, and it was love at first sight."

"Gross, I hate that love at first sight part, but it's cool how your mom found her. I hope someday my mom can find me one." Nick said.

"Guys, speaking of moms, didn't both of your mom's teach you that it was impolite to talk about someone like they aren't there, especially when they are." Addie scolded.

Martin folded his arms and said, "See, I told you Nick. Just when you think she is one of the guys, she says something like that and proves she's a girl."

Out of the corner of her eye, Addie noticed Nick looking toward the neighbor's house. She was about to ask him what he was looking at when he suddenly threw his book down and dove for the floor. He stretched his body out as flat as he could, and whispered, "Don't look at me, pretend I'm not here. Whatever you do, don't let her know I'm here."

"Who?" Addie said looking around.

"Over there, next door, the new girl Lil-l-ll-y." Nick said dragging the l's in Lilly's name out, making her sound worse than a plague.

Addie turned and looked over her shoulder at a small, very pale looking little girl with jet-black hair. The girl seemed oblivious to anything around her. As Addie watched, she slowly walked over to a rickety old picnic table that had lost any sign of paint or stain a long time ago.

When she reached the table she put one leg over the bench and plopped down like a rag doll. Turning to one side, she put her elbow up on the picnic table and leaned her whole body into the table, resting her cheek on her hand.

From where Addie was sitting, the girl seemed to be talking to herself. Addie was jolted from her observations by Martin opening the door of the gazebo. He looked down at Nick splayed against the floor, and stepped over him to get to the rocker opposite his wife.

"Addie, is he dead?" Martin asked. A half-grin emerged. "How many times do I have to tell you that neighbors are our friends?"

Nick whispered, "She didn't kill me. She's hiding me from that hideous creature next door."

"Hideous creature? Where did you hear that phrase?" Martin asked him.

"It was in one of the stories I read last night. I thought it was kind of cool," Nick whispered again. "I figured it would come in handy sometime, just not this soon."

Martin said, "Great. I bet your mother loves that phrase. Do us and yourself a favor and don't ever call your mom that, or she may insist on joining you for your reading sessions. And if she's anything like my mom was, that would seriously cut into your cookie consumption."

"Sure thing Martin, you can say that again. I would be lucky to get any cookies at all with my Mom around. Addie, is Lilly still there?"

"Yes she is, and it looks like she is talking to herself." Addie told him.

"Yeah that's her alright, probably talking to that imaginary friend of hers. The one she claims wants her to help her. How did she say it? She wants her to find her. She said this little girl is lost or something."

Addie's ears perked up at this. "Really, when was this?" She asked.

"The first day she came to school. That didn't get her off to a good start. It made her look loony if you ask me. The teacher asked her to introduce herself. That part was OK. She seemed kind of boring, but nothing strange. Then she said something that got everyone's attention. She said the little girl that use to live in that house needed her help to find her."

"Little girl? What little girl?" Martin asked.

"You said it. That's why we all call her Loony Lilly now. Because there hasn't been any little girl living in that house for like ever. When you guys moved in, that crazy man was living there. He drank too much. I remember one day I was walking past the house on my way home from the store and I heard him yelling for someone to leave him alone. When I got closer, he was laying out in his back yard just screaming. That was after his wife and little boy left him and went back to Tennessee. Do you remember Addie?"

"I remember." Addie answered shifting again to keep her gun from poking her.

"You mean he just laid there on the ground, acting weird, just like you are now?" Martin asked laughing.

"Funny," Nick said pushing himself up, resting his back against the wall of the gazebo, making sure he was still safely out of view. "Anyway, then there was, what did you use to call them Addie? Oh yeah, The Ruckus."

"Addie, is he talking about those party boys that made me call the cops on them on several occasions?" Marin asked.

"Who else?" Nick answered. "Like I said, there was no little girl around here to tell her anything. She is loony I tell you, a real goof."

Addie said, "Nick, maybe she was just trying to get attention. Maybe all she needs is a friend."

Martin shrugged his shoulders and said, "That's a good idea Addie. I think she needs a real friend. Maybe you should go introduce yourself?"

"Maybe I will." Addie said getting up from her rocker. She grabbed a napkin and a couple of cookies on her way out of the gazebo.

Nick yelled, "Hey, don't go! You might catch some weirdness or something from her, or you might…"

Martin interrupted him, "Nick my boy, you should know by now that my wife is always concerned about the underdog. There is no use trying to stop her. God made her that way for a reason."

Nick pushed himself up to a sitting position on the floor and crossed his legs, shielding his eyes from the sun with his hands. "Yeah, well tell me what's happening. I don't want to take a chance on Loony Lilly seeing me. I'm staying right down here where it's safe."

From the yard, Addie looked back over her shoulder to see Martin watching her as she crossed the grass toward the old rod iron fence. As she got closer to the girl, she could hear her softly singing. As soon as Addie heard the words that the girl was singing, she stopped dead in her tracks.

It wasn't a song with a melody, it sounded more like a child's rhyme. Addie stopped beside the fence to listen.

*Bones of Mine, Bones of Mine*
*Tied together with rags and vines*
*I am lost, yet still at home*
*Watching, waiting, till the day*
*I'll find a way, and make them pay*

13

# CHAPTER 3

From where she was standing, Addie noticed that Lilly was playing with something on the table. Lilly continued to sing the rhyme over and over to herself. Looking back toward the gazebo, Martin was giving her a look, one that said, "Well what are you waiting for? Introduce yourself."

Walking up to the fence, Addie leaned against the end post and cleared her throat. "Hello neighbor," Addie called out cheerfully, trying not to scare the little girl.

Lilly didn't acknowledge her. Not quite sure how to proceed, Addie called out again. "Excuse me, I thought maybe you would like a cookie." Addie said, crossing the yard and walking to the old table. She stopped in front of the little girl, waiting to see if Lilly would ask her to sit.

Lilly didn't respond. She simply went on singing and playing with what looked like an old book of some kind. It wasn't until Addie laid the cookies down on the table and turned to walk away, that Lilly spoke.

"My name is Lilly. Are you a mother?" Lilly asked in a firm voice.

Taken back by Lilly's question, Addie turned and looked at the girl. Lilly was still in the same position, still playing with the pages of the book. Addie walked back to the table thinking *well it's a start*. When she reached the table, she asked, "May I sit down?"

Lilly simply nodded and reached for a cookie. Not wanting to invade the child's personal space, not to mention trying to keep the rickety table from tipping, Addie walked around and took a seat opposite her.

"It's nice to meet you Lilly. My name is Addington Conroy, but everyone calls me Addie. And no, I am not a mother." Addie stopped, waiting for Lilly to respond.

Lilly straightened her back and turned her body so that she could place both elbows on the table, one on each side of the remaining cookie. She pushed her long black hair back behind her ears and stared across the table at Addie. For what seemed like a very long time to Addie, the two just sat looking at each other, as if they were each in a museum examining a painting.

This girl has a perfect poker face, Addie thought as she studied the face that was studying hers. That was when she noticed something that seemed to be just below the surface of the girl's expression. It was almost as if Lilly's face was a fish bowl, and the fish inside were looking out at Addie. Addie felt a strange sensation tingling up and down her spine. Suddenly, she felt very cold. All of the hairs on her arms stood on end. Then, in an instant, the image and the sensation were gone.

"Why aren't you a mother? You're old enough." Lilly stated, continuing to study her neighbor. "Yes I am, but my work keeps me away from home a lot, and it can be very dangerous. That wouldn't be a good situation for a child. Maybe one day I'll become a mother. Is your mother in the house? I'd like to meet her. I didn't know anyone had moved in. I didn't notice a moving van or…"

Lilly interrupted her. "I don't have a mother. She's dead, and we are not moving into this place. Not ever. My Father is renting this house for a quiet place to do his work. I come here to have lunch with him sometimes, and I wait for him here after school."

"I see. Well, he certainly picked a good spot. Nothing happens on this lane. Tell me Lilly, I'm curious, why did you ask me if I was a mother?"

"I don't have a mother. My father doesn't. I have questions that I need answered, but my dad…" Lilly said hesitantly, lowering her head in embarrassment.

*Great!* Addie thought. *I just come over here to introduce myself to a new neighbor and now I'm going to be stuck having one of those uncomfortable conversations with someone I don't even know.*

Addie felt her heart tug a bit. The girl seemed so alone, and she was motherless after all. Finally, Addie relented and said, "OK Lilly, what would you like to ask?"

"If you did have a little girl and she disappeared, would you keep looking for her?"

"Of course I would." Addie answered as her mind raced. This wasn't the question she had expected. Where was this coming from? Had this child been taken away from her mother? Maybe her mother was still alive? Before she could ask, Lilly asked her another question.

"How long?" Lilly asked.

"How long what, dear?"

"How long would you look for her?"

Addie answered with certainty in her voice and without hesitation. "Until I found her, or until I was dead."

Before Addie could say anymore Lilly nodded, stood up, and picked up the remaining cookie. She turned and walked back to her house. Addie just sat there wondering what just happened. Finally, she got up and walked back toward her yard. As soon as she neared the gazebo, she heard Nick say, "Hey, Martin."

"Yeah, what?" Martin answered pushing his Vikings cap back from his face and sitting up in the rocker.

Nick said, "Addie's coming back and she isn't bringing Loony Lilly with her. I told you she was smart."

Addie walked into the gazebo and sat down without saying a word. She had a look on her face that Nick would later refer to as the 'zombie stare'. When she turned to pick up a cookie, she noticed both of them looking at her like her face was melting.

"What?" She asked.

Nick turned to Martin and said, "See, it's just like I told you Martin, Loony Lilly affects people just by being near them. She even got to Addie. Addie looks weird. Like her body is here, but her brain is somewhere else." Nick moved himself closer to her chair. "What did she do to you Addie?"

Addie responded, "Do to me? Don't be silly. She didn't do anything to me. I was just thinking about something she said, that's all." Addie took a bite of the cookie.

"It must have been strange to shake you up like this, honey," Martin observed grabbing two cookies at a time.

Addie rolled her eyes. "Have both of you lost your minds?"

Martin swallowed before answering. "You walked in and picked up that double chocolate chip cookie and started eating it without even thinking about it. You know you've been on a detoxification diet for two weeks, remember?"

"Oh God, you're right," Addie said, wrapping up what was left of the cookie in her napkin. "I'll throw this away when we go in."

"Throw it away, no way! It's still good, you don't have bad girl germs." Nick said, grabbing the napkin out of Addie's hand.

"What is it you always say to me?" He said between huge bites, "Oh I remember, do you want to talk about it? You can tell Martin and me anything. We are both here for you," Nick added, smiling through chocolate covered teeth.

# CHAPTER 4

When Martin stopped laughing, he looked first at Nick, and then at Addie. Martin said, "Well Addie dear, at least we know he remembers something we said."

"I remember more than you think," Nick added with a pout as he folded his arms across his chest. He leaned back against the gazebo wall.

"So Addie, what did you and our new neighbor talk about? I have to admit, when you walked in you sure had a strange look on your face. Is Nick right about Lilly?"

Looking from Martin to Nick, Addie wasn't sure how she was going to describe what just happened. She wasn't sure that she understood it herself. Taking a deep breath, she decided the best way was to just tell them the truth.

"Well guys, if you must know, it was not much of a conversation. At first, I couldn't even get her to tell me her name. She just sat there, looking at me like she was studying me. I got the strangest feeling that she was trying to decide whether or not to talk to me. Then at other times, I got the impression she was more than one person. It sounds odd, but I don't know any other way to explain it."

"Yeah, that's our Lilly," Nick agreed. "I go to school with her all day. She is in three out of my four classes, so I get to watch her a lot."

"Watch her?" Martin asked. "Shouldn't you be watching the teacher instead?"

"I don't need to watch the teacher. In this school, I am so far ahead in my classes that I used to fall asleep before Lilly came along. If the teacher has the assignments written on the board when class starts, I'm finished before the class is over. Watching Lilly gives me something to do, and I get to practice that body language watching stuff that Addie is always talking about. You know, is Lilly biting her lip or does she flash a quick smirk? That could mean she is angry, showing contempt, or just loony-ness..."

Addie quickly responded, "That's enough. There is no such expression as loony-ness. I think the fact that you are watching her has a lot more to do with something other than sheer boredom, now doesn't it? It wouldn't have anything to do with your liking her just a little, now would it?"

"Oh yeah, about as much as I like my trips to the dentist, drill and all," Nick answered as he stood up.

"Come on Nick," Addie laughed. "She is not that bad."

"Yeah, but you have to admit she is creepy. And you're changing the subject that would be, what do you call it? An avoidance maneuver? Like you don't believe what you're saying completely. What did she say to you?"

Addie answered, "Remind me not to let you read any more of my profiling books. She told me her name was Lilly and asked if I was a mother."

Nick asked sternly, "And?"

"And I told her I wasn't. Then she asked me why I wasn't, since I am old enough to be a mother, and I asked her why she wanted to know. She said because she didn't have a mother, and she had a question to ask."

Before Addie could continue, Nick had put his fingers in his ears and was saying "la-la-la".

Martin pulled on Nick's arm and asked, "What in the world are you doing?"

Nick sputtered, "What do you mean what am I doing? Think about it Martin, what kind of questions do girls ask their Moms? Like I want to hear about that crap."

Martin gave Nick a stern look.

"Sorry Addie." Nick said lowering his face. "I just can't stand hearing about those woman things. I even leave the room or cover my ears when those stupid commercials come on TV."

Addie chuckled. "Don't worry Nick. I admit that was the first thing I thought of too, but that wasn't the question."

Nicks eyebrows shot up. "Really? What else could she want to know? Man, she's even weirder than I thought."

Addie answered, "She asked me if I lost my little girl, how long I would keep looking for her."

For the first time in a long time, both her husband and the neighbor boy were at a loss for words.

Finally, Nick asked, "What did you say?"

"I told her I would keep looking until I found her or until I was dead."

"What did she say to that?" Nick asked leaning closer to Addie.

"Nothing. She just got up, picked up the other cookie I'd brought, and walked back to her house without looking back or saying another word."

This time it was Martin who spoke. "You've got to be joking. That was it?"

"That's it, except for one thing," Addie answered.

"Yeah?" Nick asked. "What else?"

"During your observation times, have you noticed Lilly carrying anything unusual?" Addie asked.

"You mean like that cruddy old book she carries? That book looks like it could belong to a cave man or something."

"That's the one. She kept playing with the pages and never let it out of her hands. Not even to eat the cookie. By the way she was holding it, I couldn't get a very good look at it. Do you know what it's about, Nick?"

Nick shrugged his shoulders. "Nope, that's just another part of her loony-ness. I've got to be going guys, it's getting dark. Do you want to walk me home?"

"Sure thing," Martin said getting up, extending his hand to his wife.

Nick bounded through the gazebo door, but stopped to hold it open for his older friends. As soon as he shut the door behind him, he took his place on the other side of Addie. The three walked across the empty lot towards Nick's house.

"What's next Addie?" Nick asked.

"Next with what, Nick?" Addie teased.

Nick answered, "With Loony Lilly next door. We have to find out everything about her. We could be in danger or something. She is such a freak, who knows what she could do."

Addie shook her head. "Nick, she is just a little girl. And what appears to be a very sad, distrustful little girl. But yes, I do plan on doing a little checking. Not because I think she is up to anything, but because I am worried about her. The way she was acting, and the fact that she doesn't have a mother, worries me. I want to make sure that someone is taking care of her."

Martin asked, "You're not talking about poking your nose into our new neighbor's private affairs are you?"

"Just a little dear. Just enough to make sure that Lilly is being taken care of, that's all. I promise." Addie reassured him.

"Just a little." Nick echoed. "I'll help too, Addie. I'll keep an eye on her for you during the day. If I can, I'll try to get my hands on that book so we can take a look at it."

Addie instructed, "No you don't young man. But you can try to make friends with her. She looks like she could really use a buddy."

A frown covered Nick's face. "Yeah right, and risk my status in the hierarchy of my peers?"

"Where in God's name did you get that?" Martin chuckled.

Nick informed them, "We're studying monarchies in history class and the teacher pointed out that even in school we have what he called a pecking order. I'm one of the gentry. I can't risk that by associating with a common loon."

"Young man, the next time you come over we are going to have a long talk about social status and its lack of its importance in your young life," Martin answered, waving at Nick's mother waiting in the doorway. Nick strolled slowly off to join her, waving good night to them.

"Just think about it Nick." Addie called after him.

"I will." He answered back in the kid's tone that told her fat chance lady, unless there's something in it for me.

"Oh to be young again," Martin said as they turned to walk home. "So tell me wife, are you worried about this little girl? Cause it's not like you to even notice the neighbors, much less butt in."

"Yes husband I am, as a matter of fact. I'm very concerned about what is going on with our new little neighbor. I think I'll turn this one over to Wolff. I promise with Wolff checking them out, they won't even know he's doing it. And just to set the record straight, I do notice the neighbors. I notice everything around me, it's my job remember? Plus, I can always have the firm perform a full background if I need to."

Martin reached over, wrapped his arms around her waist, and pulled her close to him. "Well wife, did you notice your husband could use a shower? Also, I threw away that old back scrubber last week. Think you could help a guy out?"

Standing on her tiptoes to give him a kiss, she answered, "I think that could be arranged. That is if you help me out of my clothes first?"

Martin smiled looking down into his wife's grinning face. "I know that can be arranged. And I know better than to tell you no, especially when you have one of your feelings. Please do me a favor and just be careful. I don't want to see anyone get hurt," He said, bending down to kiss her on the forehead.

"I promise husband," Addie said, kissing him back on the lips.

# CHAPTER 5

The next morning, Addie was deep in thought when she walked into the office. She walked right past Holly's office, without even saying good morning. She made it all the way to her desk, plopped down in her chair, and was reaching for her empty coffee cup before she noticed Holly standing in the doorway.

"Do I dare say good morning Boss?" Holly asked, with her arms folded across her chest as she leaned against the doorframe.

"Oh Holly, I am so sorry. Good morning," Addie said getting up, while her hand was clutching the empty coffee cup.

"Here, let me get that," Holly said reaching for the cup, "Penny for your thoughts?"

"That is about all they are worth today, I'm afraid. I was thinking about a project that would be perfect for Wolff. Have you heard from him lately?" Addie asked.

"Wolff? Boy, you really are out of it today Boss. You know we hardly ever hear from him, unless he needs something or he is turning in a report. Most of the time the reports just turn up. But, if it's really important, I can try to get a hold of him. You know how much I love his voice on the phone. If I manage to find him, do you want me to try and squeeze him in between your other meetings this morning?"

"Thanks, I will let you know. I want to look at my calendar first. Actually, I really need a cup of your world famous coffee."

"I'll be right back with that coffee Boss." Holly said, shaking her head as she walked toward the lunch area.

Addie pulled up her calendar. She was thankful the business had become everything her partners had hoped for. She was only sorry that they were not here to enjoy it. Sometimes she wondered if that was somehow part of their plan all along. The more she thought about it, the more it seemed like they had completed a couple of key cases. But then it was like they suddenly let their guard down. It was as though they wanted to leave this world in a certain way, and they made it happen. That would be just like them to try and control how they went out.

The partners had worked extremely hard to establish a reputation for being the best in the business to solve certain types of cases, and now those types of cases were coming in abundantly fast. It was obvious that the firm was established with Addie and Ellis' leadership in mind. By now, the firm had doubled. Addie still missed the founders every day, even though she felt their presence near. Ellis handled the run of the mill cases, while Addie handled the more 'exotic cases', as he referred to them. By referring to them as exotic, their normal clients were not turned off by the more dangerous or paranormal side of the firm.

To Addie, there just never seemed to be enough hours in the day. The firm may have to take on another partner if her workload continued to increase. After all, someday she might just want to be a mother.

Holly came back into the room. She handed Addie the steaming cup and said, "Here you are. Do you need anything else right now? Do you want me to contact Wolff?"

Instead of answering Holly's question, Addie took a slow sip and asked, "Is this a new flavor?"

"Well, sort of." Holly grinned. "I know how much you like to start your week with a flavored brew, but the coffee delivery man has not showed up yet. We did not have enough of one flavor to make a full pot, so I combined a couple of the smaller bags."

"Which ones?" Addie asked, looking down at her coffee cup.

"You are drinking hazelnut, mint and coconut cream," Holly said proudly, as though she had just discovered a new cure for something.

"Well it's great, whatever it is. Maybe we should run out more often. Good job on the improvising. That's one of the many reasons I hired you."

Holly smiled and went back to her office. Addie looked at her online calendar and tried to find a time that Holly could squeeze Wolff into her busy schedule. She had meetings scheduled from 9:00 a.m. through lunch, and then another one was scheduled for 1:00 p.m. Addie never scheduled meetings after 2:00 p.m. She preferred to use the afternoons to make contacts and discuss assignments with her associates.

Entering a code, the next screen to come up was Wolff's calendar. As usual, only the meetings she entered were on the screen. Data entry was not one of Wolff's talents, even with voice recognition software. He would delete assignments as they were completed, but that was the extent of his communication with her. Any personal appearance from Wolff was always on his terms.

Addie had no idea when Wolff would show up next. Over the years, she'd gotten use to him finding her anytime he needed something. In other words, Wolff could see Addie at his whim, but she couldn't see him unless she scheduled it. Then again, he was one of the best freelance operatives she had ever worked with. If Wolff could not find it, then it could not be found. Period. Addie had yet to find any situation that Wolff could not handle. Entering another code, an email window opened up. Addie quickly typed a message letting Wolff know that she wanted to see him.

"Meeting in five minutes," her computer reminder her, in a seductive male voice with a soft southern drawl. *Thank God for computer geniuses with a wicked sense of humor*, she thought, grabbing her pad and heading for the conference room.

As she passed Holly's office, she asked, "Are they in the conference room?"

"Ready and waiting," Holly answered.

"Is Ellis down for this one or am I going it alone this morning?"

"He just called. He said to start without him. Ellis thinks this one is fairly routine. A resort chain wants its security system and personnel checked out by a private firm. It seems that they have had a few too many break in's lately, and the perpetrators know exactly which bungalows to hit. It sounds like an inside job."

"No problem. Do you have their bio?" Addie asked.

Holly handed her a manila folder and said, "Here you go. By the way, the facility is in Hawaii. So what do you say to the idea that we do this job ourselves Boss?"

"Maybe," Addie called over her shoulder as she flipped through the bio, heading for the conference room. As soon as she entered the room, she said, "Good morning, gentlemen." and closed the door behind her.

— — — —

For some reason Wolff was up earlier than usual this morning. He hated that. He also knew better than to even turn on the TV. The last thing he wanted to see or hear were those namby-pamby daytime people on those idiotic news shows. Coffee. Strong coffee and lots of it, was what he needed. A trip to the gym for an hour or two, and then maybe he would feel like doing something. Unless something better came up, he could use a good jolt, nothing like an adrenaline rush to start the day.

He'd just poured himself a mug of African dark roast when he heard a wolf howl coming from his computer. *Email*, he thought, *maybe this is my something better*. He called out

27

"Wolff here," activating the voice module. It had taken a long time for him to get accustomed to talking to an inanimate object. However, he liked the freedom of not having to sit behind the computer while he could be doing something else at the same time. Once the computer had verified his voice, Addie's message opened. The computer asked him if he wanted to have the message read.

"No," He answered, and walked over to read it for himself, and then read it again. *Interesting,* he thought, his eyes wide open. *Maybe I'll skip the gym.*

— — — —

Addie walked back to her office from the second meeting of the morning, with Ellis beside her. She carried the notes she had taken during the first morning meeting, which was the meeting Ellis missed.

"Looks like our schedule is picking up again," Ellis said. "I was hoping to take a sabbatical this summer, maybe take in some rock climbing. I bet you and Martin were hoping to get away, too?"

"Not this year," she answered. "We have several things we want to do around the house. Besides, I seem to have an interesting new neighbor. I'm going to have Wolff look into the situation."

"Neighbor?" Ellis asked, looking up from the notes he was reading. "What kind of neighbor would require Wolff's expertise? Do you suspect some type of criminal activity? I thought they were just a bunch of kids going for all the gusto. What is it you call them?

"The Ruckus. We called them The Ruckus, but they were asked to move out, more or less."

"So, now you have a new neighbor?"

"I have only seen the car and the little girl. She is Nick's age, eleven. She seems to be alone most of the time. She is just a little odd. I met her for the first time last evening.

About the only thing that I do know is her name, Lilly. She told me that she does not have a mother. Nick said she acts very strange in school. I just want to make sure she is alright."

Ellis followed her into her office and sat down in one of the leather wing backed chairs in front of her desk. Leaning back he just stared at her. Finally he said, "And?"

"And what?" Addie asked, leaning back in her chair.

"What do you mean, 'and what'? There has got to be more to this story than just a girl who does not have a mother and is acting a little odd. You don't expect me to believe that you would call one of our best trackers to look into an eleven-year old girl's life? Especially because an eleven-year old boy thinks she is acting strange? God Addie, all eleven-year old boys think that girls are weird. Most men think that about women as well. What is the real reason that you want Wolff to check into this situation?" He leaned forward against the desk and looked her straight in her eyes.

Addie hated when he did that. Ellis was more than a master profiler. It almost felt like he had x-ray vision. Looking straight back at him, her computer announced that she had received an email.

Ellis moaned, "Man I hate that voice thing, especially yours. Remind me to slap Talker for setting it up that way."

"Jealous that it takes my attention away from your prying?" Addie asked.

"Something like that," Ellis responded, shaking his head. "I have to get to another meeting. Whatever it is, I suppose you have your reasons." Ellis stood and walked toward the door. "Let me know what you find out."

Her next words stopped him midway to the door.

"I just hope I don't find a dead body." Addie said.

Ellis spun around to look at her. Focusing on her computer screen, she said, "Well, I guess in a few days I'll know what is going on with the new neighbors. Wolff wants to talk."

# CHAPTER 6

Addie was so busy all day that she had completely forgotten about Wolff. On her way out, she stopped by Holly's office to say goodbye, and to ask if there were any messages.

"Not a one, Boss. Looks like you took care of everything today. Did you ever hear from Wolff?" Holly asked.

"I did, sort of. He said he wanted to talk, but God only knows when or where." Addie answered.

"You can say that again. Remember when he told us he would drop off reports?"

"You mean the time you came in and they were on your desk? We couldn't figure out how he got in the office without setting off security. I remember what a stir that caused with the Captain. I miss that old man. He nearly tore the boys up that day. I thought he was going to have a stroke the way he was ranting and raving. I'd never heard anything like it."

"Well, wasn't he was a Drill Sergeant before he was promoted, back when they could still yell at the sailors? By the way, did security ever find out how Wolff did it?"

"No. To this day they have never figured it out. They begged the old man to let them use water boarding on Wolff, but he just laughed. He said if Wolff ever got mad, he would wipe out the whole bunch of them. Between you and me, I think they are still trying to figure it out," Addie said smiling.

"Addie, remember the time he dressed up like a UPS man? He came up behind me while I was filing and asked me to sign for a package. Before I could turn around he pinched me. He is lucky I didn't slug him. He's pushed his luck more than once," Holly said, grinning. "If he wasn't so damn hot…"

"Hot, is he? I am glad to see that you finally noticed. Our Wolff needs a good woman in his life. Someone he can trust that body to," Addie responded.

"I've always noticed how sexy that man is. I just figure anyone like that would never think of me in the same way," Holly said.

Addie watched how she shuffled the papers on her desk nervously. Addie teased, "Really, why not? Have you ever asked him to go out for coffee, or…anything else?"

"Me? Ask Wolff out? Oh no, I couldn't do that. What would he think?" Holly answered, her cheeks turning rosy pink.

Addie answered sternly, "Yes you can. And as for what he would think, I'll tell you. If he has half a brain, which I know he does, he would think how lucky he is that such a sweet young woman wants to spend time with him."

"Do you think so?"

"I know so." Addie answered, deciding that once she made contact with Wolff, she would make sure that he knew just how lucky he would be. Holly didn't respond, but just sat there looking down at her desk. Addie, not wanting to embarrass her any more, said goodbye and headed home.

Forty five minutes later Addie pulled into her garage, shut off the car, and grabbed a cold bottle of mineral water from the refrigerator in the garage. She started heading out towards the gazebo. When the weather was warm enough, Addie made a practice of sitting in the gazebo to unwind before Martin came home. It was a beautiful, bright sunny day. Not too cool, not too hot, it was just right. As she began walking, toward the side door, out the corner of her eye, she saw a figure pass by one of the windows at the back of the garage. A sudden rush of adrenaline hit her system. She knew two things. One, Martin wasn't home yet. And two, she wasn't alone.

She grabbed the first thing she saw on the workbench as she passed it, a piece of metal pipe that Martin had left lying there. It would do for weapon if she needed it. She did not want to pull her gun unless it was absolutely necessary. In her line of work, she has plenty of opportunities for that.

She quickly moved against the wall of the garage into the shadow of Martin's metal press. She paused as she watched and listened. She hadn't seen anyone pass the side window, but that didn't guarantee that they were not directly outside. Whoever it was could have ducked down, and could be creeping along the side of the garage.

All of the doors were shut and locked. She took a fast drink from the bottle of water. Setting the bottle down on the floor, she leaned her ear against the side door trying to hear anything that would give her a clue as to where her guest might be.

At first she heard nothing, but then a very faint crackling sound grabbed her attention. Someone was out there. It was clear to Addie that her uninvited guest was very close to the garage. A year ago, Martin had put crushed rock over her flowerbeds on three sides of the garage. The rock did not extend very far out, so whoever was out there had to be less than two feet out from the wall.

She pulled her cell phone from her blazer pocket and dialed 911 and texted a message. The dispatcher Pat answered, texting her help was on the way leave the phone on.

Everyone at the local department knew Addie's line of work only too well. Addie and her company were volunteer trainers for the local officers. They trained them in advanced hand-to-hand combat techniques and allowed them to use the company's electronic firearms training simulators. Solomon, Inc. provided the officers with training and experience that the city could never afford. In return, when Addie or any member of her team called, the city responded immediately. Addie laid the phone down and moved into position.

She reached over and turned the button on the garage doorknob, unlocking it. Using the door for a shield, she pulled it open in front of her.

Addie waited and listened. Nothing. She readied herself, holding the pipe in attack position. She heard the soft crunch again. Then she saw just the tip of a gun barrel in outstretched hands. The gun moved back and forth as the body behind it moved forward slightly. Addie waited as the intruder got closer to the doorway. Even though he wore gloves, she could tell it was a man.

Now that she was far enough in the doorway to make her move, Addie started running at lightning speed. She threw herself into the door, and at the same time brought the pipe down across the hands that were holding the gun. The intruder wailed and fell into the opposite side of the door as the gun dropped from his hand. Addie scooped up the gun, and the next moment was pointing a 45-caliber Colt M1911 pistol at one of her best operatives. He was squatting down, leaning against the doorframe, rubbing his fingers and cussing loudly.

"God damn it, Addie! What the hell are you trying to do? I think you broke one of my fingers. Give me my gun before you kill me."

Before Addie could respond, the city police car skidded into the driveway. From the Chief's point of view, he saw Addie holding a big gun over a crouching man he couldn't see clearly who it was from where he was. Slamming the car into park, Ed pulled his gun and took a ready position behind his car door, pointing his gun directly at Wolff.

"Police!" he yelled. "Put your hands behind your head and lay down on the ground."

Wolff yelled, "I am on the ground you idiot! Addie, for God's sake, you called the cops? Tell him who I am and give me back my gun."

Addie's heart continued to race as she realized that she'd gotten the upper hand over Wolff. Come to think of it, she'd never won a fight against him before. She turned and waved an OK at Ed. She flipped the gun around and handed it butt first to Wolff. Ed holstered his gun and walked toward the garage.

Addie looked apologetically at Wolff who was now on his feet, his gun holstered, still rubbing two of his fingers. Ed was the first to speak.

"So Addie, what's going on here? Is this some sort of drill or something?"

"No. Ed, this is nothing to worry about. It seems Mr. T. Wolff here thought someone was intruding in my garage. Unfortunately, at the same time I thought he was an intruder on my property. He pulled his gun and I took it away from him. Of course, I could have killed him, I might add," she said looking over at Wolff, giving him the evil eye.

"Damn straight you could have, or ruined my favorite gun," Wolff countered.

"Well for God's sake Wolff, who did you think would be in my garage? The KGB?"

Ed pointed toward his car and said, "Listen you two, what do you say we talk about this over some cookies and ice tea in the gazebo? I'll just call this in and meet you there."

Addie started walking toward the house but remembered that Pat was still on the line. She immediately retreated to the garage and grabbed her phone. Addie assured Pat that everything was fine before she clicked off. Next, she headed into the kitchen to retrieve the goodies for the boys.

Wolff was on her heels the whole time, trying to explain the reasons for his strange actions. He had been standing over the edge of Martin's steps, checking out the neighbor's lot. He wanted to find a place to position himself to watch the house tonight. He didn't see Addie drive into the garage, but as he came up the steps he'd heard a noise coming from the garage, and decided to check it out.

Addie huffed at him as she handed him the tray of glasses, napkins and cookies. She picked up a pitcher of ice tea and headed outdoors. Ed was already waiting in the gazebo along with Martin, who had just gotten home. Wolff sat the tray down on the small round table and plopped down in one of the chairs. Addie leaned over and kissed her husband hello and poured four glasses of ice tea.

"Well wife?" Martin asked as Addie sat down next to him.

"Well what?" Addie asked before taking a long sip. She was still giving Wolff her practiced evil eye.

"It's not every day that I come home to find you having a party with two good looking men. Meanwhile your poor husband has been out slaving away all day over a hot welder," Martin said, completely straight-faced.

"Well rest easy, husband, there is no party going on here." Addie added, and then chuckled a bit in response to her husband's playful jealousy.

Wolff grumbled, "That's for damn sure. I come out here at the request of my boss, model employee that I am, and she slams into me with a door. Not to mention, your wife almost broke my fingers.

"You forgot the part about her taking your gun and pointing it at you," Ed added.

Wolff spat out, "Thanks for noticing. Yeah, some party. By the way Boss, aren't you forgetting the rest of your manners? I don't think Mr. Ed and I have been formally introduced, though he looks familiar."

Addie said, "Wolff, It's not Mr. Ed. Mr. Ed was a talking horse. Chief of Police Ed should look familiar, he has been to the office countless times. He likes to visit one of our technicians in the toy room. You know the one that use to work for the police department? But if you want formalities, I can oblige. Mr. T. Wolff, I'd like to introduce you to our cities Chief of Police Ed Washington."

"Mr. T. Wolff," Ed acknowledged, "Addie, can I ask? Did Mr. Wolff just surprise you with a visit, or did you ask him to come out on assignment?"

"I asked him to look into the background of the family next door. However, I do wish Wolff would stop by the office like a normal colleague. As usual, Wolff decided to do it his way without telling anyone. Unfortunately, he failed to remember that I too am capable of surprises."

"I just thought that I would get your heart pumping. It has been quite a while since you have been out in the field. Besides, you never stand a chance against me in the gym. I do have to say though, Martin must be keeping you in good shape." Wolff stated, as though it was fact.

"Why you egotistical bas…"

"Calm down wife," Martin said tightening his hold on her to keep her from getting to Wolff, "Wolff is right, you are in great shape and I will take full credit for it."

"I should have worn my boots," Ed said trying hard not to laugh. "Addie, what is up with your neighbors? The Ruckus keeping you up at night again?

"The Ruckus was asked to leave months ago. I heard they were not paying rent or utility bills. Since then, the house has been empty. Last night I met a little girl who told me that her dad rented the place to work. There was just something not right about her, and Nick our neighbor boy, from the white house up the hill, said that she acts very strange in school. I just thought I should check it out."

"OK, so did you see any bruises or cuts or anything? Or do you think she is being neglected in some way?"

"No, Ed, nothing like that. I don't really know what it is. I can't put my finger on it. It is just a gut feeling. The other evening I went over to introduce myself to her, and she seemed very preoccupied. She almost appeared to be in a trance. She was repeating a gruesome poem over and over to herself. Then she asked me a question that gave me pause."

"What?" Ed asked.

"She asked me if I was a mother, and if my little girl was missing how long would I keep looking for her. I told her I was not a mother, but if I was, I would keep looking for my child until I found her or until I was dead," Addie answered.

Ed looked over at Wolff who was hanging on Addie's every word.

"So now what Addie?" Ed asked. "What are your plans?"

"That is where I come in, Ed," Wolff interjected, and downed the last of his tea. Wolff stood up and grabbed another cookie for the road. "That is if my boss doesn't kill me first. Martin, you have a good evening. Keep an eye on this woman, she is dangerous. Addie I will be in touch soon, from a safe distance that is. I am getting too old to be your sparring partner." He walked toward the door of the gazebo.

"I am sorry, Wolff. I was just trying to hold down the fort." Addie called after him. "I would hate to lose one of my best guys. Who, according to Holly, is very hot."

Wolff turned, touched a finger to his behind, made a sizzling sound, and winked at Addie.

"That's me, Boss. Too hot to handle, or shoot."

"Oh man, get out of here before I do decide to shoot you." Addie said.

Martin asked, "How are you leaving? I don't see that great old truck of yours."

"Parked," Wolff answered from the top of the steps. By the time Martin turned around to ask him if he could drive it again someday, Wolff was gone. Martin stood up and looked out of the back screen over the edge. There was no sign of Wolff anywhere.

"Fast, isn't he?" Addie said, taking another sip.

"How does he do that?" Ed asked, standing up to leave.

"He is in and out like a cat."

Addie answered, "More like a spook Ed. And if I tell you, I'll have to kill you."

Ed said, "I have seen your work Addie, and I'd better get back to the office. I'll do some checking on your new neighbors. You have stirred my curiosity about the little girl. You two have a wonderful evening, and don't do anything I wouldn't do." Ed walked out of the gazebo and down the path. Addie called after him, "That leaves it pretty much open Ed."

Ed just waved over his back, slipped into his squad car, and drove off.

"Well, wife, it seems like you have had a pretty rough day. What do you say we skip the cooking and go out for a bite?" Martin stood, offering his hand to his wife and helping her out of her chair. After six years together, his gentlemanly ways still made her smile. Together they carried the tray and tea into the house, after a long hot shower, they were ready to leave for dinner.

Martin asked, "So what do you think the boys will find? I sure hope there's nothing going on with that little girl."

"You know honey, I really don't know. I just have a bad feeling about all of this."

As they walked across the driveway to Martin's truck, he pointed toward the house next door. Addie turned and saw the little girl with long black hair watching them from one of the downstairs windows. Her hair hung down across one side of her face as she stared back at them with one eye visible. Even from a distance, Addie could tell that her face and rumpled pinafore were dirty.

"Is that Lilly?" Martin asked.

"No, it's not," Addie answered. "I don't know who that is."

"And look over there," Martin said pointing to the edge of the driveway. Looking in the direction he was pointing, Addie caught her breath. It looked as if the grass along the fence was alive and moving. The lawn was full of snakes. So many snakes that the grass moved like waves of water. But the creatures did not cross the property line; they slithered instead on the other side of the fence. When Addie looked back up at the window, the little girl was gone.

A shiver ran up and down her spine. What was happening seemed unreal, but Martin had seen it too. He was the one who pointed out the little girl and the snakes in the first place. All she said was, "Martin, let's go to dinner, now. I need some comfort food."

# CHAPTER 7

From his vantage point, Wolff was shielded from any-one, except the animals who knew he was a stranger. He waited and he watched. Wolff preferred to work after dark. There would be no more surprises like the one with Addie yesterday. He still could not believe he had let that happen.

Hell, maybe he was getting old. *No way*, he thought, *you only get old when you start thinking old*. His teacher had taught him that. You become what you see in your mind. In his mind, he would always be young, strong and sharp. If the time came when he could not control his mind and body, he would quit. He'd do it before he became a danger to himself, or worse, to someone else.

He scanned the perimeter, using his night goggles, be-fore looking back at the house. He peered at the upper left hand corner of the bungalow, scanning the upper window and then letting his eyes move down the side. He had just started to scan the lower level when his attention was drawn back to the small window, just under the peak of the house in the upper left corner.

What was that, some kind of light? Wolff thought. If it was, it was weird. It seemed to be coming from a single source. Why was it up there? It was brighter than a candle or a flashlight, and it had a distinct shape.

He remembered being in that house a few years back when he had been house sitting for Addie and Martin. The rock band 'The Ruckus' as Addie called them, had started in about 10:00 p.m. Lord knew he had nothing against loud rock music, but he just couldn't resist crashing the party and telling them to shut up. It was kind of fun being on the other side for a change. Normally, he was the partier. He smiled remem-bering the look on the young partiers' faces when he kicked in the front door, and stood there tapping the end of Martin's baseball bat in the palm of his hand.

He'd let The Ruckus think that they'd talked him into having a beer after they turned the music down real low. But true to his nature, while he walked through the house mingling with the guests and drinking a beer, he took mental snap shots of the interior of the house. He remembered there was a trap door to the attic in the room under that window. The same room the light was coming from.

Time for a closer look, he decided. Using the trees and buildings on Addie's property for cover, he kept a constant eye on the house as he crept along. He was half way across the yard when the light moved suddenly to one of the ground floor windows. He couldn't see anything but the light. Instantly, the light dimmed drastically.

Squatting down next to a huge oak tree, he noticed something in the grass moving around his boots. Running a gloved hand through the grass, he closed his hand around what at first felt like twigs, until he realized that the twigs were moving. Snakes. He couldn't tell how many there were, but they seemed to be everywhere. There must be a nest under the old tree. He'd check that out in the morning.

Throwing them back on the ground, he decided it was time to become a peeping Tom. Stabilizing himself against the oak tree just out of view of the window, he reached into his inside pocket. He pulled out another pair of glasses, compliments of Solomon Inc.'s toy makers. As he lifted the glasses to his eyes, he remembered when Addie had recruited him. Wolff was concerned about the company providing the kind of equipment he wanted. Everything that he liked came with a very large price tag.

They were in Jackson Square in New Orleans. He remembered how Addie simply stood and walked around behind the park bench. She'd leaned down over his shoulder and whispered in his ear in that low seductive voice of hers, "Baby, you are not in the Army any more. Not only can I get you anything you want, but I have a workshop of Santa's helpers who can make anything you can dream up." Oh, how right she'd been. Everything that she'd promised him had been more than to his satisfaction, including the payoffs. Addie had him for life, and he had a feeling that she knew it too.

Wolff lifted the glasses to his eyes and pointed them toward the window. He focused the lenses in the direction of the light. A small girl was sitting on the floor, surrounded by a pale green light. He adjusted the focus again in order to get a sharper view. The girl stopped playing and slowly lifted her head, turning toward the window. She stared directly at him. Startled by what he saw, it took a moment before his training took over again. He snapped back and started memorizing the details of the scene and the girl.

The girl didn't move. She simply sat there as though waiting for him to do something. As he continued to watch, she seemed to grow bored with watching him. She lowered her head and it looked as if she picked something up from the floor. The girl looked back in his direction one more time, smiled, and disappeared into thin air. Wolff blinked his eyes and looked back through the glasses. The only thing he saw was a dark empty room.

Pocketing the glasses, he stood and made his way back to his observation spot over the edge of the embankment. He pulled a bunch of branches and leaves over himself. He settled in with a full view of the house and yard. He held his pen-sized flashlight in his teeth as he reached inside his jacket to retrieve a pen and a small notebook He did a quick check of the house to make sure that the girl was not there. He turned to his notes and started recording everything that he could remember. Once he had finished, his notes were at least three pages long and included several sketches.

*Damn,* he thought as he turned off the flashlight and sat back against the small tree trunk. *What the hell is going on in that house?* Was this New Orleans all over again? He swore he'd never let Addie give him an assignment like that one again.

# CHAPTER 8

Addie jolted awake to the smell of coffee brewing. She rolled over and saw Martin still sleeping soundly beside her. Unless Martin had hired a maid that she knew nothing about, there was no one there to make her coffee. She rolled back again and reached for the concealed button built into her bedside table. A few seconds later, with loaded gun in hand, Addie headed toward the bedroom door.

Using the door for cover, she positioned herself to look around the edge of the door and scanned the upstairs hallway. No one was there. She left her bedroom and headed slowly down the hall to the top of the stairs. She descended the stairs quickly and headed down the hallway to the kitchen with her heart racing. As soon as she entered the kitchen doorway, with her gun positioned to shoot, she felt two large hands grab her wrists. They spun her around, grabbed the gun out of her hands, and embraced her in a suffocating bear hug. She struggled only for a moment before she looked down and recognized the hands and arms that were restraining her.

"Gotcha, Boss. If you can behave and quit pulling guns on me, I'll share my coffee with you." Wolff said.

"You already have my gun. And whose coffee is it that you're so willing to share?"

"Mine, actually. I brought my own. I only borrowed your coffee pot," Wolff answered, releasing her as he handed her gun back to her butt first. Taking the gun she looked him over. He was dressed totally in black and his face was painted like he was ready for active combat.

"Damn it, Wolff, what are you dressed for? It's a little too early to go trick or treating. And just what are you doing here on the one morning I can sleep in?" Addie scolded softly. She walked over to the kitchen island and placed the gun down on the counter.

Even as he handed her the mug, every fiber of her being wanted to shoot some part of him for making her get out of bed.

"Well Boss," he said, "Unlike you sleepy heads, I have been on the job all night. The least you could have done was dress for company. Is Martin into the grunge look? I liked you better in that number you wore when we were in Paris."

In the heat of the moment earlier, Addie had grabbed the first thing at the foot of the bed, an old pair of sweats and Martin's t-shirt.

"You're not company. There is no reason to dress up for you. And you know perfectly well, I was undercover in Paris. And whatever I wore had nothing to do with you. So, stop changing the subject. What are you doing here?" She took a long drink of coffee. She started to say something else, but her taste buds came alive. Three sips later, Martin came stumbling into the kitchen.

"Happy Saturday morning," Martin said as he accepted a cup of coffee from the commando in their kitchen.

"Good morning, Martin," Wolff said, standing near the counter.

"Good morning to you Wolff. So what brings you out so early?" Martin said, not rattled in the least by what he had walked in on.

"Work and a cup of java," Wolff answered.

"That's good," Martin answered, lifting his mug to take a drink.

Addie waited to see the look on Martin's face when he took his first drink.

Martin beamed before saying, "Wait a minute, this is good, really good coffee."

"Thanks," Wolff answered. "It's an African blend I picked up during one of the jobs your wife sent me on. Do you think it's good enough to get Addie to put her gun away? I know how much damage she can do with a lead pipe. Even though I haven't seen her shoot in a while, I do not want to find out how good her aim is. Especially now knowing what she is like when she is woken up before she wants to be."

"I would be afraid, too," Martin answered. He reached for her gun "I'll go put this away, honey." As his hands touched the gun, Addie covered his hand with hers.

"Not quite yet, sweetheart. I still haven't decided if I am going to shoot Wolff or not."

The men looked at her as if there was a small chance she that she was not kidding.

"Well, if you shoot me Addie, you will not get any more of this great coffee," Wolff said, lifting his cup.

Martin responded, "He has a good point honey."

Addie removed her hand from atop of her husbands and relented.

"Fine, put the gun away for now. But you better have something better than caffeine to share with me. Start talking Mr. T. Wolff," Addie said coldly.

Martin gingerly picked up the gun and walked over to the coffee pot. He said, "I'll just fill up my cup, go upstairs, and put the gun where it belongs while you two take care of business."

As soon as Martin left the room Wolff said, "God in heaven, you scare me woman. But I do have something important to tell you. First, however, I have some questions. I am not sure what it is I saw. It was almost as scary as you can be at times. Boss, what has been happening next door? I know that you like working on spooky stuff with other operatives, but I told you the last time - never again. Last night I saw…" He paused before saying firmly, "I want to know all that you know, no more surprises. Even if it involves what you call the supernatural."

In a quiet tone Addie answered, "Fair enough, here is what I know. No one has been able to live in that house next door for very long. In the past, there were rumors about noises and weird lights going on and off and other odd things. No one paid much attention to those tales because of the people who were making the statements. One was an old drunk. And then you met The Ruckus. Plus, the place is falling apart and should have been torn down a long time ago. It's bound to make noises and the electrical wiring has to be shot."

"And...?"

"And I didn't pay any attention until the other night when Nick started telling us about Lilly. Lilly said that they are not moving in permanently. Her father rented it to have a quiet place to work. That is one of many things that I am curious about. When Lilly started attending the same school as Nick, he said she acted strange. When I met her I could tell there was something going on with her and maybe with the house itself. I want to make sure she is not being mistreated. If she needs help, we need to get it for her. Right now, that is all I know. I have no idea if anyone is in danger or if anything supernatural is happening. What have you come up with?"

Wolff pulled his notebook from his pocket. He flipped through a page or two, stopped and handed it to Addie. "Do you know this little girl, Addie?" He asked.

Addie took the notebook and studied the sketch. "Yes, I do know her. Well, what I mean is, I don't know her name but I've seen her."

"Where, and when?" Wolff asked.

"I've only seen her once. The other night after you and Ed left, Martin and I decided to go out for dinner. As we were leaving, Martin noticed something in the grass along the fence line. It turned out to be a bunch of small snakes in the grass. We have never seen snakes around this neighborhood much, maybe one or two here and there, but never this many at one time. Then Martin saw the little girl in the window looking out at us and asked me if it was Lilly. I looked up and saw her standing in the window watching us. I told him no, it was definitely not Lilly. Then I blinked and she was gone."

The sound of Martin's footsteps came close. He entered the kitchen, dressed and ready for the day. Addie motioned him to look at the sketch she held in her hands.

Martin said, "Hey that looks like the little girl we saw the other evening. So you saw her too Wolff?"

Wolff answered, "Yeah, I not only saw her, but there is something else. Flip back a page Addie and take look at my notes."

Turning back to the previous page with Martin looking over her shoulder, Addie scanned Wolff's notes. In unison Addie and Martin looked up at Wolff from across the table and said, "Snakes?"

Addie added, "You saw the snakes too?"

"Yeah, lots of snakes. So many it looked like the ground was moving. The girl disappeared on me too, in an instant. But before that happened, I could have sworn she knew I was watching her. In fact, it felt like she was watching me," Wolff said.

Addie asked, "OK, so what is next? Where do we go from here? And why are you in my house at 5:00 a.m. on a Saturday morning?"

Wolff nodded and said, "Where we go from here is surveillance and research. As to what I am doing in your kitchen at 5:00 a.m., I needed a place to change. Plus I needed to have a good vantage point to observe and take photos now that the sun is coming up. After that, the Wolff hits the trail." He picked up the duffle at his feet and threw it over his shoulder. He stood and walked toward Addie's hallway as he called back over his shoulder, "Which bathroom do you want me to use?"

"The one at the head of the stairs on the second floor," Addie called after him.

"Let me know when I can set up the camera in your bedroom," he yelled back.

"You want to set up what in my bedroom?" Addie yelled.

He came back and stood in the doorway. "Calm down Boss, I do not want to see anything that I can't have. I need to take pictures of the comings and goings next door and your bedroom window has the best vantage point. I'll have a full view of the driveway, yard and front door."

"Then what?" Addie asked.

"Addie, let the man do his job." Martin said between bites of his cinnamon roll. "That's why you pay him the big bucks. You will get a report."

"Smart man," Wolff said, just loud enough for Martin to hear.

"Smart something," Addie grumbled, walking to her room to get dressed before Wolff walked in on her.

An hour later, Addie and Martin were ready to leave for a Saturday morning bike ride. Before they left, Wolff asked Addie to have Holly start looking into some history information for him right away Monday morning, or even sooner if she could arrange it. He wanted Holly to dig up any information she could find on the house next door, or anything else that she thought would be of interest to him.

Addie responded, "You have my permission to ask her yourself, Wolff. I would like you and Holly to get to know each other better."

"And just why is that?" Wolff asked.

"She is trying to play match maker. My wife wants everyone to be as happy as we are," Martin called over his shoulder as they rode off, leaving Wolff staring after them.

"Damn it, like I have the time for that," Wolff cussed under his breath.

# CHAPTER 9

This was the part of the job Wolff hated, setting up equipment and waiting for anything that might give him a lead.

He had to be careful not to be seen coming and going from the house during the day. There were too many retired neighbors with too much time on their hands. Of course, that was great for Addie and Martin who were at work all day. Having concerned seniors in the neighborhood made their house safer than Fort Knox. But for him, it made his job a little more challenging.

He decided to take some pictures of the neighbor's house and yard. That way, if anything changed over the next few days, he would have a frame of reference to review. As he gazed out over the yard with its trees and flowers he thought, *what a lovely area. No wonder Addie liked it so much.* From his vantage point he started snapping pictures.

— — — —

At 11:00 a.m., still sequestered in Addie's bedroom, Wolff heard a vehicle coming down the gravel lane. Wolff immediately took his position on the floor beside the window. He had his remote for the camera in hand as he leaned against the dresser. Wolff pulled back a corner of the shade ever so slightly, which would help him to decide what direction to move the camera lens that he'd mounted earlier.

What he saw from his vantage point was a red minivan, driven by a tanned white male approximately thirty-five years old. His hair was black, approximate height 5' 7', and weight around one hundred and fifty pounds. When the man stepped out of the van, Wolff noted that he wore a Khaki colored work shirt and loose fitting jeans. They looked as if they were pulled off the racks of a very exclusive outdoor outfitters store. With the door of the van opened, Wolff could see a laptop, brief case, and a bag from subway lying in the passenger's seat. He repositioned his camera and continued to snap pictures as the man went into the house. In a matter of minutes, the visitor returned to his minivan and grabbed the laptop, briefcase, and subway bag, which he brought inside. In just a few minutes, he came back out and jumped into his minivan.

Wolff clicked a shot of the license plate number as the vehicle headed down the street. He would also review the video from the cameras installed around Addie's house. There shouldn't be much if anything missed. A short time later the same van returned, this time with a little girl in the passenger seat. From the description Addie had given him, Wolff realized it was Lilly. With his camera clicking, he noticed that she was a beautiful, but sad looking little girl.

The man and the little girl went into the house, but immediately came out again carrying the fast food bag and a red and white a tablecloth. In the other hand, the man carried the ultra slim laptop. The little girl carried a tray almost as big as she was. She held it carefully out in front of her. It was filled with drinks, plates, napkins, and some kind of pastry.

Wolff watched as they crossed the yard to the broken down picnic table. He watched and listened using the sound equipment provided by Solomon, while the video recorded the session. The man flung the tablecloth up into the air, letting the wind catch it as he pulled it back down over the table. Lilly leaned over to place the tray on the table. For the first time, Wolff heard the little girl laugh.

The man looked like he was acting like a butler escorting a princess to her seat. Wolff watched as the little girl curtseyed to him in response before sitting down. The man took his place opposite her and waited as she served him from the tray that was sitting to her left. She removed a napkin, and handed one to the man first, then placed one on her lap. She removed the plates and set one down in front of each of them. She repeated the ritual with the drinks. When she was finished, the man produced the sandwiches and chips from their bag.

Wolff texted the license plate number to Holly's phone and continued his surveillance. From their high cheekbones, big dark eyes, hair, skin color, and the body build, Wolff decided they were definitely related. The man looked too old to be an older brother, which meant that Lilly had not lied to Addie about being here with her father.

Wolff watched as the two finished their lunch and put the dishes back on the tray. The man opened his laptop and arranged it so that they could both see the screen. Lilly stood up and walked to the van, and returned to the table carrying a bright pink backpack.

Lilly looked through her backpack and pulled out a very old book. *Time for a closer look*, Wolff thought while zooming in with the camera. *Much better*. He waited for Lilly to move so that he could get a good shot of the book, and then one of the computer screen. When she moved to point at something on the screen, he zoomed in to record what they were looking at. It could turn out be something useful.

Then the man nodded and rubbed his chin in a thoughtful manner, as Lilly flipped to another page and pointed to a passage. She then focused back to the computer screen. Still nodding, the man looked down at his watch and reached over and closed the laptop. When he did, Lilly closed the book and put it away in her backpack.

The two got up, and started walking to the back of the lot. Wolff grabbed the camera and headed downstairs to Addie's kitchen for a better view. They stood in their backyard, looking and pointing at something over the edge of the drop off. A few minutes later they returned to the table, picked up the lunch things, and walked back to the house. A short time later they came out, got in the van, and left.

— — — —

Once they were gone, Wolff fixed himself a sandwich followed by a couple of Addie's cookies that he found in the angel cookie jar. *Leave it to Addie to buy a cookie jar that made you feel guilty,* he thought. *Too bad it doesn't work for me. She owes me for getting me into this mess.* He grabbed four more cookies and returned to his notes.

Wolff read over what he had written. He shut his eyes and went back over the scene in his mind, making sure that he had not forgotten anything. He was almost done when something dawned on him. Flipping to the end of his notes he wrote in capital letters, NO SIGN OF SNAKES. He could not figure out why this did not occur to him until now.

Closing his notebook, he returned to the bedroom, packed up his equipment, and moved it to the third floor room at the top of the old Victorian house. From there he could put cameras up to watch both yards. He was up high enough to position a camera that looked down over the embankment. That way, if they came back later and decided to walk down the embankment to the place they were pointing at earlier, he'd catch it.

He grabbed his second bag and changed into shorts, T-Shirt, running shoes and cap. He flung one bag over his shoulder, and left through the back door. He walked quickly through the back yard, that way if anyone saw him they would never be able to identify him. Then he walked across the yard and disappeared down the steps leading over the bank. At the bottom of the steps, he looked to make sure that no one was around. He pulled back some bushes and pulled out his mountain bike. He headed down the Minnesota trails and then cut up onto a side street. His ride ended near the police station where he'd parked his truck.

— — — —

Wolff walked into the station, winking at Pat as he leaned over the desk, and asked if Ed was in.

"He sure is, but enter at your own risk. He is in one of his moods, I have to say. Are you sure I can't help you with anything?" She asked looking down at his legs all pumped up from riding.

"I wish you could, dear lady, I would much rather talk to you," Wolff answered, as he headed down the hall to Ed's office.

"You be sure to let me know if there is anything." He heard Pat say.

"You can count on that."

"Count on what?" Ed asked, looking up from a desk full of paperwork. "You flirting with my officer, Mr. Wolff? Unlike Pat, I don't get the same pleasure out of helping you."

"I don't see why not," Wolff answered. "It seems now days lots of people want to help out the Wolves."

Ed grunted, "That's Wolves not Wolff's, so quit with the wise cracks and tell me what you need."

Wolff pulled out his notebook. "I just came from watching the new neighbors next door to Addie. They are far from the type that the owner has rented to before. They come to an old run down house, sit at a picnic table that could fall apart underneath them, but conduct themselves like royalty. You know anything about who they are?"

"Not much. I was in the neighborhood later in the evening, so I talked to the neighbors that live in front of them, and then I stopped in at the Trading Post to see if I could find anything out. I asked them if they had met the new neighbors yet."

"What did they say?"

"They each told me someone had rented the house, and that they must be paying a pretty penny for the dump. I guess old Ronnie, that's the owner, stopped in at the Trading Post the day he rented it. He mentioned that if he could always rent it for the amount he just did, he was going to hold off on selling the place. He also said that he wanted to get up to the bank right away and cash their check before the guy decided it was too much."

Wolff responded, "Interesting. Let me know if you find out anymore will you Ed."

Ed said, "Why? There is no crime in renting a house for too much money, is there?"

"None at all. That is, unless they are doing more than just having picnics."

Ed mumbled, "Geez, I thought I was a suspicious old goat, but you and Addie have me beat. Poke around all you like. It's your time, and Addie's dime. Just don't cross any lines invading someone's privacy so I have to get involved, OK?"

"Yes Officer Sir. I will keep you posted."

— — — —

In his darkroom that night, surrounded by developing pictures, Wolff could not get the image of the little girl and the snakes out of his head. Standing at one of the developing trays, the first picture he finished was one of the old house by itself. What he saw riveted him. Standing in the empty driveway beside the house, looking across the yard towards Addie and Martin's bedroom window, was the little girl he had seen the night before. She was watching him do surveillance.

He stood there stunned for a moment, then he hung the picture to dry. He moved on to the next one. It was a picture of the man and Lilly at the table. Lilly was pointing to the computer screen, but beside her was the other little girl again. This time she had a hand on Lilly's shoulder, leaning over as though she were whispering in Lilly's ear. While he developed pictures, he played back the video. He was listening for the conversation and other sounds around them, not watching the screen. The only voices he heard were that of Lilly and her father. It was all small talk at first, and then talk about the area and what it had looked like years ago before there were houses.

As he continued to develop picture after picture, there she was, the ghost girl. She was in every picture except for the very last one. That was the one where the man and Lilly were looking over the bank at the back of the property. There was no little girl in sight. *So, why not this picture? Is she somehow tied to the house and immediate yard? Was she tired of being around them by that time? Who was she? Or maybe the question was, what was she?* Wolff wondered.

After he hung the last picture up to dry, he grabbed the video camera and left the darkroom. As he watched the video, one thing was very different from the pictures. There was no girl on the video, but Lilly. There was not even a change in the light.

His phone announced, "You have a text message."

It was the report on the license plate number he had texted Holly earlier. Maybe he should be the man to show her that there was more to life than just work. Then he looked at the information she'd just sent him. It was not what he had expected, but at least the man whose plates had just identified him wasn't hiding. Wolff immediately wondered what Addie would think out of this.

# CHAPTER 10

While the pictures dried, Wolff went for a three-mile run to clear his head. It didn't work. He still had more questions than he had answers. His biggest struggle was with this supernatural thing. Wolff did not believe in ghosts. The only thing that he believed in was science, and some kind of higher power.

He finished his shower and grabbed a bottle of water from the fridge. Wolff picked up his cell phone and hit speed dial.

"Detective Ed Washington," a voice said on the other end.

"Wolff here, got anything good for me?"

"Man, it is Saturday night. Unlike all of you, I have a life. Call me on Monday."

"Come on man, I know that this has to be the most exciting thing that's happened to you in years. I know this, because you have already talked to the neighbors." Wolff took another swig of water and said, "Right now, I would settle for almost anything."

"I don't have much. The truck is a rental. It was rented to a Mr. P. Brisbaux, a Canadian citizen."

"Canadian?"

Ed answered, "You heard me. I didn't stutter. It seems that he is down here on a job."

"Yeah, what kind of job?"

"Surveying," Ed answered.

Wolff asked, "Surveying for whom?"

"The county and state. Some great tracker you turned out to be, it looks like I have done your job for you." Without waiting for Wolff to answer, Ed hung up.

*Surveying for the county and state? That has to be a road project, Wolff thought. I get one question answered and three more surface.*

─ ─ ─ ─

Martin and Addie were at home, sitting in the gazebo. They had just finished a long walk along the river when Nick came riding down the gravel lane at break-neck speed. He threw down his bike in the grass and ran toward them. He was acting like he was about to announce that the world was coming to an end. He whipped open the screen door and plopped down on the floor gasping for air.      Both Addie and Martin looked at each other smiling. Then they looked at the red-faced boy whose mouth hung open.

"You wanted to say something Nick?" Martin asked.

"I sure do. Just hold on a minute," Nick answered, thumping his chest with his fist like Tarzan. "Man, I gotta get in better shape. Anyway, I've been waiting for you two to get back. I wanted to tell you guys what I found out when I was spying on Looney Lilly for you."

"For us?" Martin asked, while Addie covered her mouth trying to hold back a laugh.

"Well, it sure ain't for me. I figured it was my civic duty," Nick stated seriously.

"Civic duty?" Addie asked.

"Yeah, you know we all need to be observant neighbors. It's like that dog on TV says, so we can take a bite out of crime."

"What crime would we be talking about?" Addie asked as seriously as she could.

"I don't know yet. But whatever it is, it has to be something big. And it has to be something really old too. You know, like something from history."

"Why do you say that?" Martin asked.

"That's what I came down here to tell you guys," Nick said, looking up at them with an exasperated look. "See, on Friday our loony tunes had that old book she carries around. It was sticking out of the pocket of her backpack. Well, I sort of bumped into her, and the book sort of fell into my hands."

"Sort of fell in your hands?" Addie asked giving Nick that "Sure I just bet" stare.

"I pinky swear it did Addie," Nick answered, holding up his little finger. "Anyway, as long as it was right there in my hand safe and sound, I thought I should take a look at it before I gave it back. It wasn't like it was her diary or anything. It is way too old for that. Besides, it wasn't like I was going to keep it."

"Oh no, nothing like that." Martin added.

"Well anyway," Nick continued scowling at Martin, "I slipped it into my backpack and went to the can."

"The what?" Addie asked, once again trying to teach him not to use slang.

"OK, the boy's restroom." Nick continued. "Are you guys ever going to let me finish this story? Well, like I said, I went into one of the stalls and opened the book. It sure was old. I opened it up and what do you know? I couldn't read a thing, not one thing. It was in some kind of other language. So I kept flipping through the thing, looking for something in good old American English and what do you think I saw?"

"I am sure we have no idea," Addie added. "Suppose you tell us."

"OK, I will," Nick added indignantly. "I saw two names in English. One was Lillian, just like our Miss Loony, and the other name was Abraham Lincoln. The Abraham Lincoln, you know, the one that actor guy shot? Isn't he like your favorite President, Addie?"

"Yes, as a matter of fact he is, but how did you know that?" She didn't remember ever discussing it with Nick.

"Well, it doesn't take Sherlock Holmes to figure that out. You have a picture of him hanging in your office with two little flags on it. On your book shelf you have a little green book with his poetry in it."

"Well young man, I am very impressed with your powers of deduction. Keep this up and I may have to put you on the payroll before you are even twelve years old."

Nick beamed back up at her for a minute at a loss for words, but only for a minute. Then he recovered. "So what do you think it means, Addie?" he asked.

"Well, let's take a look at what we know. Lilly has possession of a very old book. That could mean that it has been handed down in her family. Further proof of that could be in the name Lillian. Our Lilly could be named after the Lillian in the book. Or it could mean nothing. It could be a book she found or bought at a garage sale. Maybe it's just a coincidence that there is a lady named Lillian in the book."

"So how do we find out? Do you want me to make a grab for the book again so you can have a look at it?" Nick asked excitedly.

"No. I do not want you to make a grab for the book. As a matter of fact, I do not want you to do anything at all."

"What do you mean? You're not cutting me out just when we are getting close." Nick asked, looking at her like a puppy that's just been scolded.

"I'm not cutting you out of anything Nick. As a matter of fact, I need you more than ever now," Addie assured him. "I need you to make sure that nothing happens to Lilly, or her book. I need you to do this until Mr. Wolff has a chance to give me a report on what he has found out. Will you do that for me?"

Nick nodded so hard Addie was afraid his head might fall off.

"Sure thing Addie. Will I get paid for watching her?"

"You will if you can pull it off. If you can keep Lilly and her book safe until we get to the bottom of this, you will get paid just like Mr. Wolff gets paid. How does that sound?"

"I can do that. But I want real money, and not to get

paid in cookies. I got my eye on a new skateboard and they sure don't come cheap. And, I want to help my mom pay for my tuba lessons," Nick answered, standing.

"Real money it is then," Addie assured him. "Now you say hi to your mom from me, and work on your homework. If you let your grades suffer you won't get top dollar from me."

"OK, OK," Nick agreed, getting up. He walked over to Addie and stuck out his little finger. "Pinky swear Addie?"

Addie took the oath, and they locked fingers long enough to satisfy Nick. He turned to leave, but when he got to the door he stopped short. He looked back at her over his shoulder and said. "By the way Addie, that Wolff guy is good at sneaking."

"What do you mean by that Nick?"

"I watched him on Friday night. He really does it just like in the movies. It was cool."

"How in the world did you watch him?" Addie said, looking over at Martin who just shrugged his shoulders.

"With my telescope, the one my mom got me for Christmas. I look down at the trails sometimes and watch for deer. Remember, I told you it is part of my job to be an aware citizen? Well, I saw him. I watched him until my mom made me go to bed. It sure was cool. See you guys." Nick called out as he turned and left.

Martin looked over at Addie with a smile. "Wife, I want to be there when you tell Wolff that he was busted by a kid. What do you think Abraham Lincoln has to do with anything?"

After Addie stopped laughing at the thought of Wolff conducting surveillance while he was being watched by a kid, Addie answered. "I don't know. There's only one thing that stands out in my mind that is related to this area, which involves Lincoln."

"I didn't know Lincoln had any dealings with this place. What is it?"

"He ordered the execution of over thirty Native Americans. They were hung in Mankato. It always saddens me when I think about that part of Minnesota's history."

Martin was quiet for a few minutes. Solemnly, he said. "Do you think that has something to do with our neighbors? It seems like a stretch to me."

"It does, but I want to wait and see what Wolff comes up with. Then we will go from there. I should be hearing from him in a day or two. You know that house use to belong to this property and this land. This was once all farmland. The abstract has never been updated officially. When we bought the house the insurance people caught it. I did a little digging just for fun. There are a lot of rumors about our big old Victorian lady here and what happened in this part of town."

"Really? What year was that?"

"The date on the abstract was 1870. The house next door was built in 1875, less than ten years after the hangings. That's when the properties were split, and the little house was built."

"Well, I can't wait to see what your little team comes up with. If there's a connection, they will find it. I sure wasn't expecting anything like this." Martin said standing and offering Addie his hand. "What do you say we go in? I don't know about you wife, but it has been a long day."

"Right behind you husband. I just hope we are not being watched by telescope. But just in case we are, what do you say we gross him out?" Addie said, standing on her tiptoes to give her husband a kiss.

"Hey, that works for me. Let's try that again." He said bending down kissing her again before they headed for the house.

# CHAPTER 11

Wolff tossed in his sleep. His dreams were about the house and the girl. He saw her sitting under the tree that resembled the one in the back yard, but there was no brick house.

She was sitting there with an older Native American man and a young native boy. The old man was holding up a plant of some sort for them to see. The girl would listen and then write in a book. In his dream he was watching them, but couldn't hear what they were saying. Then, all of a sudden, they all turned and looked in his direction like they could see him. Then the old man spoke and Wolff heard every word.

"Find her, so she can be with us again. We are waiting for her." The boy nodded and Wolff woke up. He sat straight up in bed and reached for his phone. The next thing her heard was Holly's sleepy voice.

"Mr. Wolff, do you have any idea what time it is?" Holly asked.

"If you're alone, drop the Mr. I need to talk to you." Wolff said.

"Alright, I am alone and now I'm awake. What is so important at 3:00 a.m.?" Holly asked.

"Has Addie asked you to find out the history of the house next door, or if anything was going on in the town around the time that it was built?"

"No. She did say that you had something you wanted me to do. Is that it?"

"Yes. To start with. See if you can find out about interactions between the local Native Americans and the white families in that area. See if there were any disappearances or any violence pertaining to a little girl around that time. Do that for me, sweet thing."

"Sweet thing? Watch yourself Wolff. If you keep calling me at this time of night, calling me names like that, I may have to do something about it," Holly warned.

"Like invite me over?" Wolff's low seductive voice asked.

"More like hang up on you." Holly answered, right before she hung up.

*Next time, I will ask her in person,* he thought. It would be much harder for her to get rid of him that way, even at 3:00 a.m.

———

Holly rolled over, wide awake. She reached for her computer pad on the night stand. God bless the boys in the shop. She was sure that she wouldn't find any connection between a little white girl and the local tribes. But there it was, in the old newspaper archives. The mayor's wife, during that time period, was very involved with the local tribes. They had a young daughter. There was a picture of the girl holding hands with a young native boy, who looked to be about the same age. As far as Holly knew, that was unheard of back then. She would have to send this picture to Wolff.

Before she got the e-mail sent, she noticed that he had downloaded some video for her to add to the case file. She started watching the video and was pleasantly surprised. How cute! A picnic with a father and daughter enjoying each other's company. Wait. What is that on the computer screen? She froze the video and zoomed in. It was in one of the articles that she had just read, She was sure of it. She reduced the screen and pulled up the archive articles again. Where was it? It was something about a local scandal. She sent the article to Wolff and told him what she had noticed.

———

This time the phone woke Wolff. Looking down at the screen, he saw that it was an e-mail from Holly. It was only 4:30 a.m. Damn, she was good at her job. He'd have to make this up to her. As he read her e-mail, he was impressed with her observations. Addie was right. There was much more to this woman that met the eye. He would have to get to know her much better. He sent a return reply thanking her, and asking her to keep digging. He told her that he would be in touch very soon.

The next morning, Wolff went directly to his darkroom. He pulled down the dry photos one by one, keeping them in order, without looking at them. He went back to his office and laid them out on his desk. Somehow, he had been hoping that the little girl would have disappeared from the photos, just like she did when he was looking at her. But there she was, on every picture.

Wolff grabbed for his cell phone.

"Hey McCoid, Wolff here. Are you busy today? I have some pictures I want you to take a look at. Yeah, I know where that is. See you about two?"

Gathering up the pictures, being careful to keep them in order, he slid them into a large envelope. He couldn't wait to show them to his old friend. Since he had time, he would do some tracking on the name and address Ed had given him. If Ed was right and this guy Brisbaux was not trying to hide, at least some part of this job would be routine.

*Time to pick up the scent*, he told himself, grabbing his duffle and the pictures as he left.

———

"Say Addie, would you do me a favor?" Holly asked, as she walked into Addie's office, setting a bowl of fruit down on Addie's desk. She sat down on the opposite side of Addie and slumped in the chair with a diet coke.

"What is going on Holly? You never drink coke this early in the morning. By the way, you look tired this morning," Addie said.

"Oh, it's not early for me. I've been up for hours."

"Oh no, what time did he call you?" Addie asked.

"3:00 a.m. But hey, he did call me sweet thing and promised to make it up to me.

"That is some consolation, I guess."

"More than that and believe me, one thing Wolff does even better than investigate is make up for his impositions, especially with women."

"That is part of the problem. I don't want to be just one of his women."

"Then you have to be the one that he can't get off his mind." Addie said, taking a bite of cantaloupe. "But this should make you feel better, I hired a partner to work with Wolff last night, only I haven't told him yet," Addie said smiling back.

Holly chocked on her diet coke. "Addie! Now I know you have lost your mind. You know that Wolff works alone. And who in God's name could you find who would even want to work with him?"

"An eleven year old boy."

"Did you say eleven?" Holly gave her a look that said Addie had just driven over the edge into Crazyville.

"Yep. I hired Nick to work with Wolff. But since I haven't seen Wolff yet, I haven't been able to tell him. It's really not as bad as it sounds. They are both going in opposite directions at the moment. Nick is watching Lilly at school, and Wolff is working on the background check."

"OK, so when do you plan on telling our Mr. Wolff that his partner is a kid? Because that is one meeting I would not mind joining," Holly said, chuckling.

Addie answered, "When the trails that they are both working on start to come together, I'll let Wolff know. Until then, I think I'll just let them wander off in their own directions."

"Well Boss, you are either a genius, or you are nuts. I am not sure which, but I'll play along and keep your secret. But, you have to let me be there when you tell Wolff. What do you say?"

Addie grinned. "Sure, why not if I can? Who knows I may need some back up."

"Yeah, or someone to hide behind is more like it." Holly added with another giggle. Standing up to head back to her office, she asked one last question. "So if you hired Nick, do I put him on the payroll?" She asked, as seriously as she could.

Addie answered, "As a matter of fact yes. That is if you can figure out a way to do it without getting us in trouble with child labor laws. He wants to be paid with real money. He informed me last night that he wants to buy a new skateboard, and help his mom pay for his tuba lessons. I promised him that he would be paid officially. I'll have him fill out a real time sheet."

"OK. I'll talk to Earl in accounting." Holly called back over her shoulder, shaking her head.

———

It only took Wolff a couple of phone calls to find out that Mr. Brisbaux wasn't just any surveyor. He'd actually been hired by the State of Minnesota to work on a citywide development plan for revamping city, county, and state roads. Wolff had no trouble finding out from Lisa at city hall what Mr. Brisbaux's schedule was for the rest of the week. He pretended to be an Electrical Engineer that was scheduled to have a meeting with Mr. Brisbaux, *this is way too easy*, he thought. *Then again, something had to be*.

Wolff spent an hour watching and listening to Brisbaux on the job. Sure enough, he appeared to be hard at work planning a new city park along the river. Everything Wolff saw and heard appeared to be normal. He decided to follow Brisbaux. Something just didn't fit about him, even if his job was legit. There was something other than the disappearing little girl that was strange. There just had to be more to the story.

— — — —

McCoid's face lit up at the sight of his old friend, as he came up over the green. Seeing Wolff again made Mac feel like he was back on the job. Wolff was sitting serenely at one of the clubs many outdoor tables. True to form, Wolff had chosen a table off to one end where he could see the entire outdoor dining area. *Just in case*, Mac thought as he crossed the patio, motioning for Wolff to stay seated. Pulling off his golf gloves, he reached across the table to shake Wolff's hand, and then pulled out a chair for himself.

"God it's good to see you again Mac," Wolff said. "Looks like retirement agrees with you."

"It sure does kid, that is if guys like you would let me be retired. What is so important that it brings you to a golf course in the middle of the day? It can't be just to say hi or shoot the bull."

"Nor is it these watered down drinks," Wolff said, pushing his aside.

"So spill it, kid. What is it?" Mac asked, motioning to the waiter to bring two more scotches this time it would be from his private locker.

Wolff smirked and slid the envelope across the table to Mac. He leaned back in his chair. "You tell me man, you're the expert."

Mac reached for the envelope. He removed the pictures, and laid them out on the table in front of him. Picking them up, he examined each one closely before putting them back down. He didn't say a word when the waiter returned with his drink, he just accepted it without comment. He sat back in his chair and took a long, slow sip, still looking down at the pictures in front of him.

Finally Mac looked Wolff straight in the eye and said, "So what's the deal kid? How did you make these? How did you get these double exposures to look like this?"

"That's just it Mac, I didn't do anything. I just snapped regular pictures and when I developed them there she was, just like you see her."

"Yeah right, what kind of joke is this? Why did you bring these to me, you giving out jobs to retired forensic photographers?"

"No," Wolff said leaning forward tapping one of the pictures. "But you're the only Forensic photographer I know who could tell me what caused this. I want you to tell me that there is a perfectly rational explanation. Cause if you can't man, there is only one other explanation."

"Yeah, what's that?" Mac asked, taking another drink and realizing this was no game. His young friend had a look in his eyes that he'd never seen before. It wasn't fear. His friend looked like he was actually spooked.

Wolff said, "This time, I am not the only watcher. While I am watching my subject, she is watching me."

Mac answered, "Let's not jump to any conclusions until we check it out. First things first, finish your drink. Then, if you want me to, I'll check out your camera and the negatives that go with these pictures. If I don't find anything, you can take me to where you took these and let me have a look around. I have to admit though, weird is not the only word for these pictures," he said, picking up another one and tilting it into the light. "Just look at this little girl, you can even see the outline of the style of dress. It's very old, like a picture from the early 1900s or before. All I have to say is that you had better not be pulling my chain. Cause if you are kid, let me tell you. I may be old, but I can still out shoot you."

Wolff set down his empty glass, leaned over and whispered, "God, I hope it is some kind of trick Mac. Cause if it's real, I have finally found something that can scare me." Wolff answered.

# CHAPTER 12

Addie and Martin were seated in the library room of their favorite local restaurant. Each room of the restaurant featured a different theme. Being surrounded by books made Addie feel at home, not to mention from her seat she could see anyone coming her way. She felt her cell phone vibrate. Sighing, she reached for it. She thought it was like trying to grab a live fish in her pocket. She hated cell phones. Then again, they did keep her in constant contact with her operatives, which was much safer.

She glanced at the screen, clicked it on and asked, "Where are you? Do you have some new information for me?"

"I am feeding the ducks," Wolff answered.

"Feeding the what? Addie said, looking over at Martin who was waving at someone through the restaurant window. He turned back to Addie and leaning forward, Addie could see the figure of a man near the edge of the pond. Sure enough, it was Wolff. He held a bag in one hand and a cell phone in the other. Gathered around his feet were geese and ducks of all sizes.

Addie said, "Would you care to join us? Or would you rather hang around with your bird friends?"

Wolff answered, "Nah, birds are too flighty for me. Kind of like women, I would love to join you and Martin, if it's not a special occasion."

"No special occasion. I'll tell our waiter that we need the room to ourselves for a while."

Martin was grinning from ear to ear. Addie motioned for her favorite waiter, John, as he walked past the library doors. She picked up the wine list. If she had any doubt about having wine with dinner, there was no doubt now. If Wolff was joining them, she'd more than likely need a bottle.

Addie had just finished ordering a bottle of wine when Wolff appeared behind John. Wolff pulled up his own chair at the end of the table, positioning himself to see the full length of the room.

"Good choice of a restaurant," Wolff said approvingly.

"Glad you like it," Addie said.

Martin interjected, "I love feeding the ducks at the pond. I usually take them cat food. They digest it better." Addie knew Martin was trying to keep the conversation light.

Wolff cleared his throat. "I thought I should bring you up to date."

"That's so nice of you, and it's even more considerate that you are doing it at dinner time and not at 3:00 a.m." Addie said.

Wolff gave Addie a half grin. "I called Holly sweet thing. That didn't work out like I planned, but you know I will make it up to her some way. I think you were right Addie, I need to take a closer look at our Miss Holly. But back to business, you should know that Mac may be sending you an invoice as well."

"Mac, as in McCoid?" Addie asked looking puzzled. "I thought he was retired. Wasn't he a forensic photographer?"

"Yes and yes," Wolff answered, grabbing for the bottle of wine in the waiter's hand. "I'll take that. How soon before you bring those world famous popovers?"

John headed back out of the room as he mumbled that he would get them right away. Before Addie could object, Wolff had the bottle opened and was pouring a glass for the three of them.

"Well?" Addie demanded.

Wolff answered, "Oh, yes where was I? I remember now, Mac. Well, I had to call him. It seems that there is either something wrong with my camera, or we need an exorcist."

Now Wolff had Addie's full attention. She asked, "A what? Wait a minute, first you tell me you need to hire a forensic photographer and then you tell me we need an exorcist? How about you just give me your report. Remember, I'm the boss. I'm the one who decides who we need to hire," she reminded him.

"Yes, Sir," Wolff answered with a salute and a wink. Martin turned toward the window and tried to hide his smile with his hand.

"Well, let's see," Wolff said pulling out his notebook. "I found out about your neighbors. At least the two of them who are actually alive. First, the man and the girl are father and daughter. They are from a prominent family in Canada. And I do mean prominent, like he doesn't need to work prominent. Their names are Louis Chadwick Brisbaux and Lillian Lores Brisbaux. Louis is a widower. He has been hired by the state as some kind of special planner. Everyone that I've talked to on the job site speaks very highly of him, and his work.

They come to the house during the day to eat lunch. After school, Lilly comes home and hangs around until her father gets off work. When he arrives, they leave and go back to a very plush townhouse on the other side of town. Why he has rented the house and has her wait there for him after school, I have no idea."

The waiter appeared with a fresh basket of warm popovers. Addie took one and said, "Interesting. Keep digging, I want to know everything you can find out about him." She smothered the roll with honey butter.

Wolff said, "Way ahead of you Boss. I am waiting on some more information to come in from a contact in Canada. That brings us to Mac and the second little girl who is still nameless. That is unless we take into account the information Holly found. Take a look at these." Wolff pulled a stack of pictures out of his jacket pocket and handed them to Addie. When Addie and Martin finished flipping through the pictures, he asked, "Now do you see why I need Mac?"

Addie handed the pictures back to him and asked, "So you did see her again? And you were able to take pictures of her? What did Holly find?"

"Not exactly," Wolff said, while pocketing the pictures. "Her image showed up in the pictures after they were developed. That's why I called Mac. I'll let you know what he comes up with. In the meantime, Holly found this." He handed a printed copy of an old newspaper article about a missing little girl with a picture. "Maybe you should prepare for an exorcism. Maybe one of those weirdoes that you worked with at that metaphysical place could help us out."

"They're not weirdoes," both Addie and Martin answered simultaneously.

"OK, OK," Wolff said, holding up his hands in surrender. "Forget I said anything. I just thought that you may want to be prepared. From where I stand, I think the little girl in the newspaper and the one in my pictures, are the same girl. Fictional ghosts like the ones in Ghostbusters I can handle, but this kind? I want this settled because now even I am having dreams about this kid. God knows I don't mind dreaming about young women, but I prefer them to not only be of age, but to also be alive."

Addie said, "I'll give them a call tomorrow."

Wolff poured another glass of wine and said, "Great! Now let's eat. I'm starving. All this sneaking around makes me hungry."

"Wolff, breathing makes you hungry," Addie added. "Do one more thing, when you are checking, look to see if there is any kind of link between our Mr. Brisbaux and Abraham Lincoln."

Wolff's eyebrow shot up. "Abraham Lincoln? What would he have to do with this?"

Addie answered, "Well, your junior partner thinks that there is a connection, so check."

"My junior what?" Wolff demanded.

"Your partner, Nick. My eleven year old reading buddy," Addie said sitting back, waiting for the news to sink in before she added, "I wouldn't want you to think that you were the only one that could hire additional personnel. And don't say anything. He is already on the payroll."

Wolff grunted and leaned back in his chair swirling the wine in his glass, waiting for Addie to continue.

Addie continued, "As I was saying, Nick got a look at that old book Lilly carries with her. He said it was written in another language, now knowing that they are from Canada, I suspect it's French. However, Nick was able to pick out two names, Lillian and Abraham Lincoln."

Leaning forward and looking Addie in the eye, Wolff said very coolly, "Yeah, well you had better warn him, He may be in for a rougher ride than just working with me."

"Really, what makes you say that?" Addie asked concerned.

Wolff answered, "I don't know how to explain it. Hell, I don't know how to explain any of this. It seems to me that this little ghost of a girl is able to communicate with our Miss Lilly. It also seems as if she needs Lilly to do something for her. Do you have any idea what would happen if Nicky boy comes between the supernatural and the natural? Or what might happen if he distracts Lilly from what the little girl needs her to do? The ghost girl could strike out at Nick, or do something to keep him away. Remember New Orleans Addie."

"Point taken," Addie said looking over at Martin.

Martin added, "Addie, you know young entities do act out in childish ways sometimes. They are still children after all."

"You are right about that, husband," Addie agreed.

Wolff interjected, "I don't know anything about that stuff. Hell, I haven't decided if I even believe there is such a thing. But I do have two pictures of her with her arm around Lilly's shoulder. In one, she looks like she's whispering in Lilly's ear and pointing something out to her. In the other, she still has her arm around Lilly's shoulder, but she is looking back at me and she is not smiling. It's as though she is watching to see if I'll try to get closer."

"It's almost the same way a guard dog watches you approach. A good one doesn't bark right away, he just stares with a fierce, warning look. But if you cross that invisible line only that dog can see, you are dead meat. That is the kind of feeling that I got from the little girl." Wolff popped a piece of popover into his mouth. He used the last of it to clean the remaining pasta sauce off of his plate. Draining his wine glass, he stood to leave.

"Thanks for the warning, Wolff," Addie called after him. Wolff turned around and gave Addie another little salute. As he passed by the waiter, he shoved a twenty in his lapel pocket and was gone.

Martin said, "So, wife, do you think we should make a call to Father Joseph tomorrow and see what he thinks about all of this?"

John was standing next to him, holding a large desert tray filled with goodies. Martin pointed to a huge piece of caramel apple pie, knowing the waiter would know to heap on the cinnamon ice cream.

"I was thinking more like calling him tonight," Addie answered, pointing to a piece of chocolate mint cake." She smiled up at the waiter and said, "John, would you pack up a piece of this to go? And please bring me a cup of coffee while Martin finishes his pie."

# CHAPTER 13

"I ate too much, but it was so good," Martin said, as they walked across the restaurant parking lot to their car.

"Me too. All I want to do now is spend a quiet evening at home with my husband. What do you say I challenge you to a game of dominos, Mister?" Addie teased.

"I say no way, it's not fair. You know how I am after a big meal like this. You'll beat me. How about we watch the Travel Channel and plan our next vacation? Maybe they will have one of those haunted bed and breakfast things you like. Then we can write down ideas of where we would like to go. That is, if I can stay awake."

"Oh, does that mean you have already decided we should go somewhere soon?" she asked.

"The sooner the better. Somewhere that we haven't been before, and somewhere alone," Martin answered.

"You're on. We'll watch the show and first thing Monday morning, I'll have Holly start looking up possible locations. I am not going to take a chance on you changing your mind this time," Addie told him, as they drove towards home.

"Me change my mind? Who's the one always putting it off for the next big case?" He took one hand off the wheel and pointed. "Hey, what is going on down there?"

Turning in the direction he was staring, Addie noticed three squad cars. Two of them were in their driveway, and one was blocking the entry to the lane that ran in front of their house. Martin continued down the street to a second entrance to the lane that ran down the hill. He parked next to a small store called the Trading Post. One of his neighbors was standing outside, transfixed by the events happening in front of her.

"Hey neighbor," Marla said, as Martin and Addie stepped out of the car. "Is there something that you might

77

want to tell your neighbors about the two of you?" Marla was the daughter of the Trading Post's owner. She pointed toward the police cars parked outside their home.

"I was hoping you could tell me," Martin answered. "We went out to dinner at Dangerfield's, so what is going on?"

Marla said, "All I know is that I was getting ready to close up when dad heard the address come over the police radio. I guess one of the other neighbors heard a disturbance in the brick house next to yours. From what we heard, it seems like vandals were breaking out windows. They were yelling at someone inside the house."

"The police arrived. Even the Chief of Police, Ed Washington. We saw Nick with his mom and grandpa go running down to the house. Maybe they were the ones who called it in. A few minutes after the cops got here, that man who rents it drove up in that state pickup truck. It's the brown one down there. Did you know he worked for the state Martin?"

"We just found out," Martin answered. "Do you mind if I leave our car in your lot? It looks like my driveway is going to be occupied for a while."

"Sure thing. Let me know what you find out, and if you need any help just give us a call." Marla said. Martin and Addie locked the car and took their time walking down the lane to the house.

They had just started to cross the back yard when they heard Nick's voice calling to them from the gazebo.

"Hey Martin and Addie, we're over here."

They headed for the gazebo only to find Lilly sitting in one of the rockers. A paramedic was fussing over her while Nick and his mother stood next to her. They could see that Lilly had the start of a black eye, and a large cut on her head.

"See what you can do here, wife. I'll go find out what's going on," Martin said, heading for the crowd at the end of his driveway.

"I hope you don't mind us using your gazebo," the paramedic said. "We want to get her to the hospital as soon as possible, but she refuses to leave without her father."

"Don't worry about that," Addie answered. "Nick, take my keys and go open the house. Let's get Lilly inside where they can get a better look at her head until they can take her in the ambulance."

"No!" Lilly screeched. "Not without my papa."

"OK, OK honey, let's get you inside. When your dad's here, he can decide what he wants to do," Addie said, walking beside the paramedic as he carried the little girl toward the house. Once inside, the men took a look at the bump on Lilly's head. Her shiner, as Nick put it, was growing around her eye under the ice pack.

Addie could see that the paramedic's ice pack was getting warm. She reached into her freezer, pulled out another one, and handed it to the paramedic. Then, she directed them down the hall to the family room. Nick followed close behind, not letting them out of his sight. Nick sat down on a footstool next to Lilly and the paramedic. Totally out of character, Nick reached for Lilly's hand. She didn't pull back. Instead, she just looked over at him with the faintest of smiles.

When Addie returned to the kitchen, she saw Nick's mother Laurie making microwave popcorn and putting cookies on a plate. It was obvious that in times of stress, Laurie fed people. In Addie's house, everyone made themselves at home.

"Help yourself to a drink, Laurie," Addie said. "Do you know what happened?"

"All I know," Laurie said, reaching for a diet Pepsi in the fridge, "is that I was in the kitchen making supper when

Nick came downstairs screaming that there was trouble at the brick house, and asking me to call 911. He tore out the back door and nearly gave me a heart attack."

"Grandpa ran after Nick. I dropped what I was doing, shut off the stove, and grabbed the phone. By the time I got down there, Nick and his grandfather were yelling at some big kids who were running away from the house. That's when I noticed some of the windows were broken. The next thing I knew my dad was carrying Lilly out of the house. I couldn't get her to tell me anything. By then, the police arrived. Then the brown pickup truck pulled up and Lilly yelled for her dad, but called him Papa. The police stopped him immediately to talk to him. I told her that she had to wait until he was done speaking with the police. That was when you showed up, and that's all I know."

Addie said, "Well teasing her at school for being different is one thing, but destroying property and harming her is quite another. That won't be tolerated in this neighborhood. We'll give the surveillance tapes to Ed and let him get to the bottom of it. Whoever they are, they picked the wrong neighborhood if they were expecting to get away with it." Addie said, grabbing a handful of popcorn.

"No need for that Addie," Nick said coming back to the kitchen. "I know them all. They're kids from my school. They have been going after her almost since day one, but I never thought they would go this far."

"You know who did this?" Addie asked.

"Sure I do," Nick answered. "I was watching them from my bedroom window with my telescope. I saw them sneaking around the house for almost an hour. Then I heard them yell something, but I was too far away to hear what it was. When I looked back through my telescope, I saw them picking up rocks. One of them picked up a log from Martin's woodpile, and a couple of them had old bricks that they found in the yard. All of a sudden they started throwing them at the house, and that's when I tore down the stairs and told mom to call the cops."

"Police officers son, not cops," his mother corrected.

Nick just huffed.

Before Addie could ask the names of the boys, the back door opened. Suddenly the kitchen was full of men, and they all seemed to be reaching for the popcorn and cookies at the same time.

Addie watched as Lilly's father made his way through the men. "Where is my little girl? Did they bring her in here?" From the family room down the hall they heard Lilly squeal.

"Right this way Sir." Addie said, leading him down the hall to his daughter.

As soon as Mr. Brisbaux reached her, he scooped her up in his arms and she held tightly to him.

"My little flower," he said in a strong French accent. He stroked her long black hair as he rocked back and forth. "Are you alright little one?"

Addie walked over to them, laying a hand on the man's arm. She said quietly in her professional tone, "I think Lilly needs to go to the hospital."

Mr. Brisbaux nodded. He agreed and set her down on the gurney that the paramedic had rolled in. He kissed his daughter on the forehead, and she obediently lay backward allowing them to take care of her.

Addie tightened her grip on his arm. "Sir, you go ahead and go to the hospital with her. My husband and I will meet you there. That is, unless you would like one of us to drive you?" Addie asked.

He told them that he had left the work site in such a hurry, his truck was still there. The one outside belonged to the city, and it needed to go back to the site.

"Not to worry," Martin answered. "If there is one thing we always have plenty of around here, its vehicles."

"Ain't that the truth," Officer Ed said, "Sir, we are going to have to ask you some questions, as well as young Nick here. We'll follow all of you to the hospital."

"Oh good God in heaven Nick, now what have you gone and gotten yourself into?" Nick's grandpa scowled.

"Addie, you tell him that I was just doing my job," Nick answered, bolting up from his seat. "Aren't you the one who is always telling me to get a job? Well, I did. I went out and got myself a job. I work for Addie now, and I'm an investigator," Nick said, standing up as tall as he could, looking straight into his grandfather's dumfounded face.

"Is that true Miss Addie?" Nick's grandfather asked, when he had recovered from the shock.

"True as true can be," Addie answered. "I may have to cut the check to his mom though, with child labor laws being what they are. Nick is on the job, and given what happened here tonight, he may have saved Lilly's life. Who knows just how out of hand this could have gotten."

"Well, I'll be damned," his grandfather answered. "Good job Nick."

Suddenly, Lilly said something in French and the room became quiet. Her father nodded and kissed her cheek in response.

"What did she say?" Nick asked in a whisper.

Bending down over his daughter, Lilly's father translated his daughter's message for Nick. "She says that she is Lucky Lilly now, because you were there to save her."

"What does she mean by that?" Nick asked.

"It is a long story my boy, a very long story and right now we should go to the hospital," the man answered. He followed the gurney to the door.

"I'll follow Mr. Brisbaux and get the truck back to the site, and then I will bring him to the hospital, honey. You follow with Nick and his mom," Martin said, as he fell in behind the paramedics.

"No. I want to ride in the police car." Nick said, as he looked over at Officer Ed.

Nick's grandfather scolded him, "Hey there young man, you watch your mouth. Just because you work now don't mean you can be disrespectful."

"Yes sir. May I please ride with you, Officer Ed?" Nick asked.

"Sure Nick, you're a hero now." Ed answered. "I might even let you turn on the siren."

"Cool!" Nick said, as he headed for the door.

"Meet you there," Addie called after them. She and Laurie locked up the house, and headed for the car.

# CHAPTER 14

At the hospital, the ladies found Martin leaning back in one of the ultra-comfortable chairs in the hospital's waiting room.

"He will be asleep in no time," Addie said to Laurie, who nodded in agreement.

Nick, on the other hand, was pacing back and forth across the room like an expectant father, stopping once in a while to take a gulp of Coke.

"Young man, where did you get that?" Laurie demanded, tapping one foot on the floor while giving him the mother look.

"Officer Ed," Nick stated confidently. "You don't want me to offend Officer Ed by declining his offer, now do you? If you and Addie hadn't taken so long getting here, you could have said no for me."

"Never mind, I don't have the energy to argue with you now." Laurie said slumping down in a chair on the other side of Martin. He didn't even seem to notice.

"Have you heard anything yet Nick?" Addie asked, grabbing a bottle of water from the small fridge provided by the hospital.

"Nope, not a word. Why do you think I'm so nervous?"

"She will be alright. Thanks to you and your Grandpa's quick action. By the way, where is your Grandpa anyway?" Addie asked looking around.

Nick answered, "He stayed home. Gramps told Officer Ed if he wanted to talk to him, he would be at home watching Wheel of Fortune," Nick answered.

Addie asked, "I take it Officer Ed is in with Lilly and her father?"

"Yeah, she calls him Papa though, not dad or anything. It seems weird, but I guess that's how they talk in Canada."

"You're right about that. My family is French on my father's side, and he always called his father Papa." Addie answered.

"No Sh…?"

Laurie interrupted, "No what?"

"No kidding," Nick said, looking sheepish at his mother.

Before she could say anymore, voices came from the hall behind them. They turned to see Officer Ed and Mr. Brisbaux walking toward them. As they got closer, Addie knew the look on Ed's face. There was little room for misunderstanding. He was angry.

"Mr. Brisbaux, this is a very serious situation we have here. Those young men need to be taught a lesson. Sir, your daughter could have been killed tonight. The city will press charges on the boys. I would appreciate your cooperation in this matter. Do you understand?"

"Yes Officer, I understand. But what I don't understand are the actions of these young men. Why would they attack Lilly and throw rocks at her, like she was a dog? My daughter has always been so quiet. She didn't provoke them in any way that you know of, did she?"

Ed said, "No Sir. Maybe Nick can shed some light on what went on tonight." Ed looked down at Nick, who was standing between the two men hanging on every word.

"Who me?" Nick answered.

Kneeling down, he looked Nick in the eye. Mr. Brisbaux asked softly, "Nick, is there any reason that you know of that would cause these boys to go after my little girl? If so, please tell me."

Nick stuttered, "Well, well…. cause she's weird."

"Weird? What are you talking about? I don't understand," Mr. Brisbaux looked confused.

Addie interrupted, trying to soften the words. "I think what he is trying to say is that the other children think Lilly is a little different. It seems that the children think Lilly acts strangely because she is not making friends with any of them. And the fact that she is always reading a tattered, old book that she doesn't want anyone else to see. They noticed her hanging around the old house by herself. The children took that as strange behavior, and started to make up all kinds of stories. That is what kids normally do to new kids."

"Yeah, but she is kind of loony," Nick muttered.

"Loony? As in lunatic?" Mr. Brisbaux asked.

"I suppose he does mean that," Addie answered. "But don't forget now, he is just a kid too."

"Oh no, that can't be. It can't be happening again, not to my Lilly." Mr. Brisbaux stood, shaking his head in disbelief.

Ed demanded, "What do you mean happening again? Has this kind of thing happened to Lilly before? Were the same kids involved?"

"No, I misspoke. It didn't happen to Lilly. But there has been a little girl harmed before, and I believe it was in very close proximity to the house where Lilly was attached," Mr. Brisbaux answered.

Ed said, "I know you have had a rough night and you want to get back to your daughter, but as soon as possible, you and I are going to have to talk about what you just said. In fact, we have a few other things we need to talk about too. Understand?"

"I do," Mr. Brisbaux said. Addie could tell by his body language that he was exhausted. Addie asked, "Mr. Brisbaux, may I make a couple of suggestions?"

"Yes Madame."

"Please call me Addie. I own a private security business and…"

"I know Madame. When I traced the house I had a firm such as yours investigate all the neighbors. They have already suggested that I call on you and your firm if anything should happen. I would like very much to engage your services."

"Fair enough Mr. Brisbaux. I believe you just confirmed that you are here doing a bit more than a job for the state. We'll be happy to accommodate your business in any way that we can. I must warn you, we don't come cheap," Addie said.

"I have also heard that. Then again, I would not expect the best to be cheap. I believe I can pay your price, and I have it on good authority that you are the best. How should we proceed?"

Addie said, "First, I would like to call one of my operatives to act as personnel protection, at least for tonight. Then you and Lilly can rest easy. Tomorrow morning after you and Lilly have had a chance to rest, and Officer Ed has had a chance to talk to our bullies, we will all sit down and talk this over. Maybe once we know what is going on, we will be able to help you and Lilly with whatever it is that you are trying to accomplish. What do you say, Sir?"

"I say call me Louis, and I accept your proposal." he answered, looking relieved.

"Good, let me make a call and I will have one of my operatives here within the hour." Addie said.

Addie walked a few feet away so she could make the call in private. She was able to reach Tan. He was an operative that she had used many times. She told him that she needed his protection expertise as soon as possible, for at least 48 hours. An hour later Addie, Marin, Nick and his mother left the hospital with Officer Ed. Tan arrived and had been briefed on the situation. He was in place outside Lilly's hospital room, where the girl was fast asleep. Her father was in a chair next to her, dozing off as he watched the early news.

"Thanks for bringing in your man, Addie," Ed said, as he zipped up his jacket.

"I don't have an officer that I can spare right now, and I don't want anything happening, not until I find out what the hell is going on."

"Those are my thoughts too, Ed." Addie answered.

"I could have stayed with Lilly. I can protect her," Nick said, kicking at the sidewalk in front of him.

Addie said, "I know you could have, but I need you watching the neighborhood. Not to mention the fact that you are a minor. I'm not allowed to work you too many hours per day." Addie teased, as she reached over and tossed his hair.

"Is that true? I can't work twenty four hours a day if I want?" Nick asked looking at Martin.

"Has Addie ever lied to you?" Martin asked him.

"Only once," Nick answered.

"Nicholas!" his mother scolded.

"She did mom. One time she told me she made cookies without any calories."

"You got me there Nick." Addie laughed. "But that's a lie I tell myself every time I make them. I'd forgotten that I told you that too. Do me a favor Nick, go home and get some sleep while you can. I have a feeling I am going to work you hard on this case."

"You got it Boss," Nick called over his shoulder, as he ran for the squad car. He stood right next to the passenger side, letting Ed know that he expected a ride home.

"Me too?" Martin asked, looking over at Ed.

"Martin, you have our car," Addie reminded him.

Ed said, "Thank God. I don't think I could handle the two of you. But Nick, no sirens this time. It's too late for all that noise."

"Cool, see you at home," Nick said, giving his mom a quick wave as he got into the squad car before Officer Ed could change his mind.

"Man, I wish I would have left the car at home," Martin mumbled, kissing Addie before climbing into their car. "See you at home ladies." He called out the window as he followed the police car out of the parking lot.

"I guess boys are always boys and they never grow up, do they?" Laurie asked Addie.

"Not if we're lucky," Addie said as she reached her car and unlocked the doors.

# CHAPTER 15

During the ride home from the hospital, Addie asked Laurie if she would mind if Nick missed a day of school tomorrow. Addie explained that she'd like to have her and Nick come to the office. He could take part in the meeting with Mr. Brisbaux, Lilly, Officer Ed and her operatives.

"I think Nick would love that, but why do you want him?" Laurie asked.

Addie said, "For one thing, it would be a good learning experience for both of the kids. Secondly, it may put Mr. Brisbaux, or at least Lilly, at ease to have Nick there. She'll need a friend her own age. She has grown to trust Nick and that may make both of them more cooperative. The sooner we put this matter to rest the better, before anything else happens. I've also had it on my to-do list for a long time to make arrangements with the school to start a neighborhood watch program with the kids. We could start by focusing on bullying. This is the perfect opportunity to set it up. I want to avoid another incident like tonight."

"I think that's a great idea. What time do you want us ready?" Laurie asked.

"Nine would be fine. I'll take you and Nick into the office with me. I'm sure it will take Mr. Brisbaux awhile to get Lilly checked out. I'll have Tan bring them into the office. Holly can set a 10:30 meeting up with Ed if he can make it."

Laurie said, "I don't know who is going to be more excited, Nick or me. I hardly ever get out of the house, much less be part of a meeting."

"Watch out with the fun part. I may put you to work too," Addie teased.

When they pulled into the driveway, Nick was already there, standing next to the squad car. He rushed to his mother's side of the car and opened her door. At the same time, Martin opened Addie's.

"What took you two so long?" Nick goaded.

"We had to obey the traffic laws, unlike you all who go through intersections with a flash of lights," Addie answered.

Nick interjected, "None of that happens on Officer Ed's watch. He just took the short cuts."

Addie said, "You'll have to show me those someday." She smiled up at Martin and then turned to Ed, who was leaning against the squad. "Actually, Laurie and I were talking on the way home about a meeting tomorrow. I was going to have Holly call by but since you're here, one less thing for her to do."

"Yeah, how do you want that to go down Addie?" Ed asked.

"I'd like to do it at our office. I'll have Holly set it up as an official taping of the testimony. You can bring whoever you need, or let Holly know tomorrow morning if you need a court reporter or anything else to make it official."

"I'll bring what I need. What time do you want me there?" Ed asked.

"10:30?"

"Addie, you know my blood sugar. By the time I drive to your office, it'll cut right into both my break times. Throws me off for the whole day,"

"I remember Ed, don't worry. Holly will order your favorite bagels and one of those Ruben's from down the street that you like so much. You can take it with you for the ride back. I don't want the city coming after my company for altering the blood sugar of one of its executive officers."

Ed said, "You are a good citizen Addie. I'll see you tomorrow. I hope when I get back to the department the guys have those little punks in custody. We can try and figure out why they felt they had to do what they did. By the way, if the parents give me any grief, I am thinking that you've got a camera on that side of the house. We may need to prove to them what their sons are capable of."

"As a matter of fact, we do. Ever since The Ruckus lived there, we've had a camera pointed at the front half of the house and another one on the garage, which has a view of the back yard of the little house. Not to mention a couple more cameras that Wolff put up the other day. I would bet that we caught those young men from almost every angle. If you want one of the disks, come back to the house with us. You can have it."

Ed nodded in agreement.

"Hey, wait a minute. He is getting bagels tomorrow morning Addie? What about me?" Nick asked.

Addie bent down to whisper in Nick's ear, "when you get there you can help Holly order them and you can get first pick even before he arrives."

"For sure? How am I going to get there? It's too far to ride my bike," Nick said, looking like someone who had just been told that he had won the lottery.

"I'll tell you all about it while you are getting ready for bed, young man," Laurie said, pointing him toward home.

"Bed? I can't sleep yet, I'm wide awake," Nick said.

Laurie put her hand on his shoulders and turned him toward home.

Martin said, "Wife, what do you say we get the video for Ed? Then we can go to bed too. I'm bushed."

"Husband, I say that sounds like a plan," Addie answered. "That is as soon as I make of a couple of calls to Holly and Wolff about the meeting tomorrow. I need him and his forensic photographer there if possible."

"Any reason why they wouldn't come?" Martin asked.

"That's the question I always ask myself about Wolff. But then I remember that Wolff and most of his friends march to God knows what kind of drummer, just like ghosts don't always show up when we want them to."

———

Wolff had just gotten comfortable after scanning his notebook and sending the notes to Addie. "Sometimes I thank God for technology, but then again..." he said out loud. Between his handwritten notes, what he kept in the locked box of his brain, and the pictures he had taken, he was sure that he had covered all the bases he could for now. Suddenly, he heard the wolf call coming through his phone. "Wolff here," he said, as he waited for the seductive female voice to answer.

"Good evening Mr. Wolff, the boss is calling." Some people had simple ring tones. That would have been far too simple for the boys in the shop. *Then again, at least they left vibrate alone.* Wolff thought.

"Hey Boss, husband fall asleep on you so you need a little Wolff time?"

"Sorry, no Wolff time needed here. What I do need is you and Mac tomorrow morning at the office at 10:30 a.m." Addie didn't wait for Wolff to object or redirect, she simply hung up.

Wolff smiled at the thought of Addie hanging up. She knew he always wanted to be the first to end the call. He would have to change it up a little, since obviously he was becoming too predictable. He phoned Mac and asked him if he had finished his examination of the pictures and equipment. Mac assured him that everything had checked out fine. Mac even made a trip to the house in question to have a look around. There was nothing out of the ordinary, and he couldn't find any sign of snakes.

Mac said, "I took some shots of my own, using my equipment."

Wolff asked, "And?"

Mac answered, "And nothing. No snakes, no little girl, just an empty little brick house. I didn't even get any of those weird balls of light. What is it the ghost hunters call them, Orbs?"

"Orbs, yeah. No nothing? Are you sure?"

"Yep," Mac answered. "Maybe the ghost girl doesn't like me or something."

"Maybe," Wolff answered. "Can you make it to a meeting at the office tomorrow at 10:30 a.m. and bring everything with you?"

"You bet. I haven't seen Addie or Holly in ages."

"Good, see you then."

— — — —

When Ed got back to the station, he found the parents of the vandals sitting, and pacing around the room. *This is the fullest the waiting room has ever been*, Ed thought, as he walked in the front door.

One of the parents saw Ed and immediately jumped up. Mr. Paulson said, "Ed, what on earth is going on here? What is the meaning of having your guys come to my house and tell me that my boy is locked up for questioning?"

"Ours too." another father said, standing and walking over to Ed, coming way too close for comfort. Ed knew he was in intimidation mode, and it was way too late for that.

Ed said, "Back off and sit down both of you. I'm going to check on a conference room where we can talk in private."

As soon as they were all in the conference room, Ed sat looking at the tired, angry parents. He knew all of the adults and their boys. They were good upstanding citizens and, until now, there had been no trouble with any of the boys. *Oh well, better get this over with, the sooner the better.*

94

Ed said, "I don't know how else to say it, so I'll just come right out with it. Tonight, your boys were involved in a vicious, dangerous incident on Riverside Lane."

Mr. Paulson huffed, "Riverside Lane? There isn't anything down there anymore. What would our boys be doing on that Street? This must be a mistake."

Ed replied, "Sorry Mark, there is no mistake. You all know Addie Conroy. She is the one with the private security firm downtown. She has security cameras all around her place." Ed pulled a flash drive from his pocket and held it up in the air, "Here is the video from tonight. All three of the boys are all over it."

Another father said, "You still haven't told us what they did to get themselves arrested."

Ed said, "I'm getting to it. To begin with, they vandalized 711 Riverside Lane. They threw rocks, bricks and wood at the windows."

Paulson smirked before saying, "That old brick house next to the Conroy's? Who cares? That place has been empty for almost a year. Furthermore, it should have been condemned years ago. I would think Addie would be happy if something happened to the old place. The property value on the whole block would go up. Don't you guys agree?" He asked, turning to the other fathers.

Ed said, "It doesn't matter if any of us agree that the house should be demolished or not. It is still private property. Your kids just can't go around throwing stuff at it. But that is not all. The second charge they are all facing is assault."

Paulson spat out, "Assault? What the hell are you talking about? Who was assaulted?"

Ed answered, "A little girl by the name of Lilly Brisbaux. Her father rents that house, and she was inside when the boys started throwing the rocks and bricks. It seems that they weren't only after the house, but wanted to get at Lilly as well."

Paulson said, "That is insane. I don't know who this Lilly is, but my boy has never been in any kind of trouble. And he would never throw rocks at a little girl. Why would they do that? Maybe they didn't know she was inside?"

Ed replied, "They knew she was there and they were taunting her from outside before they started to throw objects at the house. I am hoping that the boys will tell us why. By the way, I just came from the hospital. Lilly was hit in the head. They are keeping her overnight. We should know more in the morning. Now, It's getting late and I know all of you have to go to work in the morning, so your boys will be here until we find out how Lilly is doing, at least for tonight. I suggest you get lawyers. Tell your lawyers that I would appreciate it if your boys would simply tell us what made them do this. Remember, this is not a matter of them denying it, we have it all recorded. What we need to know is why they did it."

"Well I for one don't care how late it is. I am not going home or getting a lawyer or doing anything else until I see for myself," Larry insisted.

Ed sighed, walked over to the computer, and slid in the flash drive. What the parents saw shocked them. The time was 7:00 p.m. recorded by the surveillance device. There was enough light to clearly see everything. Lilly was sitting at a broken down picnic table. Suddenly there was a noise from over the embankment. From the surveillance it was hard to hear exactly what was said, but it was obvious by the look on her face Lilly was afraid. She jumped up and ran for the house. She was acting like she knew who was coming and why. The next minute the boys came over the top into the yard, moving toward the house.

Lilly was already inside when they reached the back yard. They couldn't see her. When the boys got close to the house, they all stopped short. They acted like they saw something that terrified them. Then, they heard Micah Olson say, "Oh no you won't! You won't get us. We'll get you first!" Then the boys picked up whatever was close at hand and heaved it at the house as they retreated over the hill toward the river trails below.

After that, Ed shut off the monitor and said, "My officers found your boys not far from the house on the side of the river. They had a bonfire going and were all sitting there like nothing happened. They refused to answer any questions, so we brought them in. You want to talk to your sons now?" The parents just sat there, nodding.

# CHAPTER 16

*Now it's Holly's turn to deal with him*, Addie thought as she, Nick and his mom walked into the agency the next morning. Nick had talked non-stop all the way in. But now, Nick would have Holly to talk to. Nick ran ahead and was already perched on the corner of Holly's desk, talking away by the time Addie and Laurie passed her office.

"Nicholas," his mother scolded. "What have I always told you about sitting on furniture that was not meant to be sat on?"

Nick said, "You say tables are for glasses, not asses."

Laurie looked embarrassed. She mumbled, "You could have left the last part out."

"But you asked," Nick said, trying to hide a grin.

"It's alright Nick," Holly said coming to his rescue. "Your mom was just trying to keep you from losing your job."

"Yeah right, I just started," Nick said, nonetheless looking concerned.

Holly said, "Well, if someone were to come in and see you sitting on the edge of my desk, they may take it the wrong way. They might think that you were trying to harass me or something. After all, you are an operative and I am nowhere near you level with the company."

Nick jumped off the desk. He said, "Oh right, we learned about that in school. It's like no pulling the girls hair or hitting them too hard in dodge ball."

"That's right." Holly answered, "When we are in the office we have to act professionally, no funny business."

"OK," Nick answered. "So what do you want me to do?"

"How about going over this list with me? You can pick out the bagel flavors. Then we'll walk down to the deli and buy them."

Nick said, "Yeah, that's way better than letting them be delivered. We gotta make sure that they are fresh, maybe even warm. We don't want any old left over ones cause Lilly's going to be at this meeting." Nick took the list and pen from Holly and began checking off flavors.

"Lilly?" Holly asked. "Nick, you wouldn't be getting personally involved with a client would you?"

Nick looked over at her with a bewildered look on his face as if to say this is going to be a long day.

"Oh brother," Addie said, walking toward her office and motioning for Laurie to follow. She asked if she could get Laurie anything.

"Some tea would be nice," Laurie answered.

As soon as they entered Addie's office, she pointed toward a chair. "Have a seat and I'll grab you some tea. Do you like peach? Holly found this wonderful cinnamon peach tea the other day."

Laurie nodded smiling and sat down on a plush wing backed chair. This was the first time that she had been there, but it had a familiar feel to her. The room reminded her of Addie in every way. The colors of the room, the furniture and the old world look. Dark wood halfway up the walls and the antique walnut desk were all things she'd choose. Not to mention the mementoes scattered around the room from many of the places Addie had talked about.

"Here we are," Addie said, handing Laurie a cup of tea and sitting down opposite her in the other wing backed chair.

"Your office is lovely, Addie," Laurie said, "It's hard to believe that this is the office of an investigator. That is what you call yourself, isn't it? I guess I never asked you."

"Close enough," Addie answered, "We call ourselves security consultants. The corporation was originally started by three men who retired from the military. I had worked for one of them when I was in the Navy, when he was involved in research."

"Was that Ellis?" Laurie asked.

"No. The man who hired me died a couple of years ago. As a matter of fact, there is only one of the original partners still living. Ellis and I are the second generation who were recruited by the founders. Who knows, Nick may be part of the third generation. He seems to be a natural, and the help seems to like him," Addie said, laughing out loud.

"Where Nicholas is concerned, you never know," Laurie responded.

"You never know what?" Nick broke in.

"Know about you, son. I never know about you," Laurie answered.

"Well, Grandpa will be happy to know that I am doing what he told me to do," Nick said.

"And that would be?" Addie asked.

"He said when it comes to women, to keep them guessing," Nick answered walking toward the door, leaving the two women smiling at each other behind him.

"Are you guys coming to the meeting or what? Lilly's waiting." Nick called over his shoulder.

"Right behind you," Addie called back.

Laurie said, "Remind me on the way home that I need to have another talk with Grandpa, will you Addie?"

"I think that would be a good idea." Addie grabbed for a file on her desk and followed Laurie out of the office.

"They are waiting for you in the conference room, Boss. That is, everyone except for Wolff," Holly announced.

"Now there's a surprise. I hope he makes a normal entrance. I don't want to put our clients through any more,"

Addie said, opening the door of the conference room for Laurie. "Please show him in when he gets here."

"Will do."

The door hadn't completely closed behind them when Addie heard Wolff's voice coming from the outer office.

"You will do what?" He asked, passing Holly and grabbing for the half-closed door. "Sorry I'm late," he said, walking over to Nick and sticking out his hand. "You must be my new partner. Nick, is it?"

"Yes Sir," he answered, reaching out to shake Wolff's hand with a grip that surprised the older man.

"Nick it is," Wolff said, introducing Mac.

"Please, everyone help yourselves to breakfast. I think it's time we get started," Addie said. She watched Nick hand a bagel to Lilly. Then he patted her shoulder as he took the seat beside her, smiling at her the entire time. Addie was so amused it was all she could do to continue.

Once they were all seated, Addie went around the room introducing everyone, leaving Lilly and her father for last.

Addie addressed him, "Louis, Why don't you introduce yourself and your daughter. Part of the reason we are having this meeting is because we know so little about the two of you and why you are here."

"Thank you," Louis answered, leaning on the table as he addressed the group. "I am Louis Chadwick Brisbaux and this is my daughter Lillian Lores Brisbaux. We are from Quebec. I am, by profession, a civil engineer as well as an architect. I applied for a position in your state. Not for the job itself, even though I am finding it to be most enjoyable. I took it because I believe Lillian and I have another tie to your city. That is to say, one of our ancestors did. We have come here to attempt to right a wrong."

Ed interrupted, "What kind of wrong are we talking about?"

"We believe it was murder. One that was never closed. How would you say it? It's a cold case?" Louis asked.

"Are you talking about a murder in my city? When and who do you think was murdered, Mr. Brisbaux?" Ed asked setting down his bagel.

"A young girl. The year would have been approximately 1862."

# CHAPTER 17

"1862 Mr. Brisbaux? This case of yours brings new meaning to the words cold case, don't you think? More like something from the ice age?" Ed asked. It was obvious he wasn't buying any of this.

Addie intervened. She said gently, "Ed, now that Mr. Brisbaux has introduced himself and his daughter, what do you say we introduce ourselves before we get into the details of the case."

Ed answered, "Sure thing. It's not like we have to be in a rush or anything, since it's already been over a hundred years." He slouched back and folded his arms across his chest.

"Thank you," Addie answered, "Louis, we tend to go on a first name basis here if that's alright with you?"

Louis answered, "Yes, please."

"Good, call me Addie."

Ed said, "You can even call me Eddie, if it would make you feel all warm and fuzzy." The officer said while reaching for his bagel. Ed was letting his guard down just enough for Addie to poke him in the ribs.

"Louis," Addie continued without skipping a beat, "What we do here is security of all kinds. From reviewing security systems to personnel protection, as well as transfer of shall we say sensitive materials from one place to another or from a seller to a buyer. Occasionally, we take on a missing person's case. However, they are not the usual missing person cases, and we have been known to use some creative means to find someone."

Wolff chuckled, "Creative, I like that. I'll have to remember it."

"Case and point," Addie said pointing at Wolff. "Mr. T. Wolff is an operative that we subcontract for some of our more difficult cases. So far, he's found everyone that he has been asked to locate. And everyone that he has been asked to protect, lived while under his watch. Before I turn the floor over to Wolff, do you have any questions for us?"

"Only one. You said Wolff has found everyone that he has looked for, but can he find one that is no longer with us?"

Addie answered, "Yes, I think he can. That is, with some help from one of our other associates. Actually, I have asked one of them Marie, to join us by phone."

Louis rubbed his forehead with his fingertips as though he was in pain. "I don't totally understand. As the officer has pointed out, she has been missing for over 100 years. What makes you so sure your company can find her?"

"Yeah Addie, I would like to know the answer to that one too." Ed said sarcastically.

"She just told you, she has the best men on the trail." Wolff answered confidently, tapping Mac on his shoulder. Both of them leaned inward, grinning at Ed.

Addie added, "I'll tell you Ed, I don't think she will be as hard to find as you think. But, I would like to talk to Marie first. I want her to talk to Lilly. I have a feeling once we hear more of Lilly's story and we take a look at some of the evidence Wolff and Mac have already collected, we may have more to go on than you think."

Ed took a small recorder out of his pocket and placed it on the table in front of Louis. He said, "In the meantime, what do you say we all come back down to earth and hear some of this evidence you have? Tell us about this missing little girl and how your family is connected." Ed pushed the button on the recorder.

All eyes turned to Louis, pens in hand, prepared to take notes. That is except for Wolff and Mac.

"As I have already told you, there was a young girl murdered or at least that was the rumor. Her body was never found. I don't believe my ancestor killed her, but I have come to believe that she was killed as a result of her relationship to him. My ancestor was the Native American Chief that your city was named for. He was my great, great grandfather." Louis said, looking over at Addie.

"You are related to Chief Eatoshaka?" Addie asked.

"Yes." Louis answered.

"I never was very big on history." Ed said, "But isn't he the guy they hauled back from Canada to hang because they thought he killed this little girl?"

Louis shook his head. "No. They never found the little girl or any evidence that he was involved with her disappearance. He was hung for his supposed involvement with the Native American uprising in your state."

Ed said, "So, you are not sure that there was a murder? And you got no body either, just a belief? So why the hell do you care? Is it messing up your good family name or something?" Ed slammed his fist on the table in frustration.

Addie said, "Louis, I think what Ed is trying to say is, you seem to have gone to a lot of expense and trouble over something that happened so long ago. And now you are telling us that you don't even know if this little girl was murdered?"

"Lillian Elizabeth Tyrickson was her name."

"Hey, another Lilly," Nick added, as though he had just woken up.

Lilly said in a quiet tone, "I am named after her."

"My mother named me after her. She told me she thought it might make Elizabeth happy to know that we remembered her," Lilly answered.

"OK, so we maybe have a murder or we maybe do not. And then there is the little fact that it's older than dirt." Ed interjected.

Addie rolled her eyes at Ed. She said, "Louis, please continue with your story."

"Yeah, by all means continue before my batteries die in my recorder," Ed said, sitting back in his chair like he was getting ready to watch an old movie.

Louis cleared his throat and continued, "I know how strange this sounds. But to my wife, as well as several of the women in my family, it is very real. In fact, they believed what happened back then caused their premature deaths. On her deathbed, my wife begged me to find out what really happened to Elizabeth. She was convinced that unless the truth is known and every effort is made to make some kind of restitution, our Lilly would suffer and die early just like she did."

Wolff asked, "Sir, why did your wife believe that her illness and death were connected to something that happened 100 years ago?"

"It's a long story, as you can see from this book," Louis answered, holding the old book up for everyone to see. "The book contains the last words of the Chief Eatoshaka, as well as his wife and several of the women from my family. They believed they had been cursed." Louis went on to explain the Chief's friendship with the Tyrickson family,

'The owner of the only general store in the small riverside town believed in living peacefully with the Native Americans in the area. He established a very good barter system with the Natives that proved to mutually beneficial for the whole town.

It seems the Chief's wife and oldest daughter were especially close friends to Elizabeth's mother. The Chief's daughter and Elizabeth's mother were pregnant at the same time. The Chief's daughter delivered a fine healthy boy, and the next day Elizabeth's mother went into labor. Unlike her friend, her baby was breach and the doctor would never reach them in time. The Chief's wife begged Elizabeth's father to let her help her friend, his wife. His wife begged him to let the woman come and help her. She did, and was successful. She not only saved Elizabeth, but saved the mother too.

Elizabeth's father was forever in their debt and the families were united even more. Elizabeth and Two Ponies, the Chief's grandson, being only a day apart in age, grew up together. The entries in the journal say that both mothers knew how much the young boy loved his little friend. That was a source of concern for both women, especially when they saw how attached Elizabeth was to him. He was always waiting to walk her home and carry her books after school, which was a school that he was not allowed to attend. The two would go to a spot they liked on the riverbank, and Elizabeth would teach him everything she had learned that day in school.

In return, Two Ponies and his grandfather, the Chief, would teach Elizabeth the native ways. The Chief was sure that someday the two of them would be able to bring peace between the tribes and the white man. If these two could be so close and live in peace and harmony, they all could. At least, that was his dream.

Then one day some of the other boys in school followed Elizabeth home. It seemed that she had shunned a prominent young man's advances, and he was determined to know why. They saw her meet Two Ponies and followed them to their place by the river. They watched in horror as he read a poem to her that he had written for her in perfect English.

From Elizabeth's account, the boys jumped Two Ponies and started to beat him while yelling obscenities. Elizabeth ran to her home and brought back her father, who scared them all away and brought Two

Ponies back to his family. Elizabeth's father paid for medical care for Two Ponies, who among other small injuries had a broken arm. The tribe was grateful to Elizabeth, but from that time on knew the she and Two Ponies would have to meet in secret if they were to continue their friendship. It was too dangerous for them not to.

From that day on, Elizabeth would sneak away any time she could while her mother rested and her father was busy with his store. She would go through the woods to the back of the camp, and Two Ponies would be waiting to let her into their teepee. They would never allow themselves to be seen together.

One day, the Chief asked Elizabeth how she could come so often, and if her mother and father didn't miss her. Elizabeth explained that her mother had grown very tired and spent much of her time sleeping, and her father was always at the store. Without her mother able to help out at the store, her father was busy all the time. A few months later, the Chief received news from town that Elizabeth's mother was deathly ill. He went with his wife after dark to the house. Elizabeth's father brought them in to see his wife.

The Chief left some medicine with Elizabeth, and instructed her to make a tea from the roots and leaves for her mother. Her mother's recovery was remarkable, that is until the local doctor found the tea that Elizabeth was giving her. He took the herbs and forbid her to ever give it to her mother again. Her mother worsened each day and a month later died.

When the news reached the tribe, they mourned her loss as one of their own. They stayed away from the funeral until everyone was gone. Then they went to the grave to pay their respects while the sun set. Later that night, Elizabeth went to the tribe. She begged the Chief's wife to let her stay with them. Instead, they took her back to her father who from that day on, doted on his daughter until another woman came into his life. When news of the upcoming wedding reached the Chief, he asked Elizabeth about her new mother and the girl answered, "She is not my mother. She said she sealed a deal with my father, whatever that means. Sometimes I think she hates me." The Chief recalls how he took her by the shoulders and looked down into her sweet, but sad face. He assured her that a mother never hates her child, even a stepmother. "Her words pained me to my soul." He remembered when she turned and said the words, "I think if my father was not here, she would kill me."

The Chief took her into the teepee and Two Ponies looked up and smiled to see her. She stayed close, watching everything he did, and asking questions now and then. She stayed as she had done so often for the evening meal, and then Two Ponies walked her to the edge of the woods behind her house and waited until she was safely inside the old Victorian they had called the painted lady.

According to the chief, after her father married her stepmother, Elizabeth came more often. He was intrigued by her fascination with the plants and flowers of the area that they used as medicine. He wrote that she was wise beyond her years. She use to follow them around while they gathered herbs and wild flowers for his medicines. He said she also had a book that she carried. In it she wrote down what he told her, and drew pictures of the plants. When he asked her why she was writing it down, she told him she wanted to grow up and be just like him, a Chief of her people.

Then one evening at dusk, Elizabeth came to see Two Ponies. She brought a book so big that she could barely carry it. Two Ponies' mother came to the Chief and expressed her concern for her son. The two children had taken the book and left camp, heading toward the river. When they did not return by dark, the tribal braves went looking for them. They found Two Ponies a couple of hours later sitting by the river, staring straight ahead. He didn't have the book, and Elizabeth wasn't with him.

The Chief ordered the boy to be put to bed, and they would call a meeting in the morning to determine what to do. The next morning, before the Chief had a chance to talk with Two Ponies, two braves stumbled in to tell the Chief about their involvement with the murders of the settlers in Northern Minnesota. The uprising led to Eatoshaka running from the Army to Canada. Shortly after the Chief ran, his wife was arrested. She did not survive the interrogation. The details of what happened to her were not listed, as he was never able to find out exactly what had happened.

When word reached the Chief, he grieved the loss of his wife terribly. It was during that time when one of his new friends, who had been working with the tribes, felt sorry for him and asked him to come to stay with them for a while. He was hoping to learn from him, as well as protect him. My great, great grandmother was the younger sister of the man who befriended the Chief. The Chief and my great, great grandmother fell in love and married in a private ceremony at my family's home in Canada. She was pregnant with their child when he was arrested and brought back to Minnesota. She followed him back, and rented a small house to be close to him.

The Chief stood trial, but while he was being held in prison Mr. Tyrickson came to see him. He told him of his daughter's disappearance and begged him to reveal any information that he could. He said that Elizabeth's stepmother was wasting away having lost Elizabeth. He said that she couldn't have any children of her own, and was devastated.

The Chief was severely heartbroken. His first wife was dead, his grandson had not spoken since the day they found him by the river, and now he'd found out that Elizabeth had been missing since that same night. He swore he knew nothing, but promised to write down everything that he could remember about the last few days before he left the country. He hoped that something he remembered could be used to find out what had happened that night between Elizabeth and his grandson.

For the next several days, he told his wife everything he could about the days before he left. She recorded it all in this book along with thoughts of her own after each visit. He had her bring Two Ponies, now a young brave, to visit him. He tried to get the boy to tell him what had happened, but Two Ponies offered him nothing. When the Chief pressed him to tell him anything he could about that night and mentioned Elizabeth's name, the young man's eyes turned wild. He jumped up from the chair and ran from the jail. When the Chief's hanging day had finally arrived, his wife, who was almost ready to deliver their baby, insisted that Two Ponies be there.

Louis continued; allow me to read my great, great grandmother's words. Today, my husband was led to the gallows. Elizabeth's stepmother Mrs. Tyrickson, shouted for him to tell her what had happened to Elizabeth. Of course he couldn't tell her, he didn't know. He could only stand there, a dirty, thick rope wrapped around his neck. He refused a hood for his head and told his hangman he wanted the last thing he saw on earth to be his wife and child. With tears running down his cheeks, he watched as Mrs. Tyrickson pointed to me and screamed a curse on the future women of our family.

The moment the woman finished screaming her curse, my water broke. I dropped to my knees in heavy labor. Looking up at my husband's face one last time, I watched the hangman pull the lever. I screamed in pain and anger looking back at Mrs. Tyrickson, but I could not bring myself to hate her. The look on her face was that of a woman whose soul had already left her body. As another wave of pain ripped at my belly, she broke away from her husband and ran toward the river-bank. Before anyone could stop her she screamed and threw herself into the river.

I was carried to the doctor's house and gave birth to our son. I remember waking to see my husband's spirit standing next to my bed, looking down at me smiling. I heard him say, "You have given me a fine son, my wife. Please find Elizabeth, bring her home, and plant wild flowers for her." I promised him I would do everything I could to find her. Now being a mother myself, I could not imagine losing my child. Then I felt his lips brush my cheeks, and I fell asleep.

When I woke up, Two Ponies was standing next to my son's cradle, singing a song that my husband used to sing to me. When he saw that I was awake, he turned and ran. The next day, I learned that Elizabeth's mother had drowned. She was 29 years old.'

When Louis finished, he stopped and closed the book. He stared at the cover for a minute without saying anything. The room was silent for a few moments before Ed asked, "I still don't see why you are here now, trying to solve this disappearance. Good God man, what good will it do? Even if you can find something, it sure won't bring any of them back."

"Ed, for heaven's sake." Addie scolded.

"Or maybe there is something else in it for your family that you haven't gotten around to telling us yet?" Ed demanded.

Wolff shouted out, "Hey man, you don't have to talk to the poor guy like that. We came here to hear him out. Besides, it is his right to search anything in his family's past if he wants to. And quite frankly, this is the most interesting case I have worked on since New Orleans."

Before anyone could say anything else, Lilly jumped up and ran to the door crying. Nick ran after her with his mother close behind, shooting the officer a sharp look as she said, "Now see what you did, you made Lilly cry."

Staring coldly at Ed, Lilly's father said, "Sir, I assure you I do have a purpose in solving this crime."

Addie pleaded, "Then please Louis, tell us. Nick and his mother will take care of Lilly for now."

"The reason is very simple." His voice cracked with emotion as he tried to continue. "I am honoring my late wife's last request. I am hoping that if we find Elizabeth Tyrickson and bring her home, it will put end to the suffering of the women in my family. I need to stop the curse that Mrs. Tyrickson pronounced that day. And it doesn't seem to matter if they are born to my family or marry into it. If they are the first wife to one of my decedents, they die before the age of 30. If they are the first daughters, they die before the age of 14.

Lilly and I are the last of the direct descendent of Eatoshaka. This is the first time since the day he was hung, that there has been a first wife who has given birth to a first daughter. Just like Mrs. Tyrickson and her daughter. Don't you see, my wife died at age 29 of a rare lung disease that caused her to drowned on her own fluids. The doctors told me there's no known cause of the disease and no treatment. My Lilly is 11, and in three years, she will be..." He stopped, rubbing his forehead hard enough to make his skin slightly red. "Coming here, trying to find the answer is my last hope to try and save my daughter. She is all I have left, she is my whole world."

# CHAPTER 18

"Man, this beats all I've ever heard. OK Louis, so you want us to do what exactly?" Officer Ed asked.

Before Louis could answer, Holly poked her head in the door.

"Addie, I have Marie on video conference. Do you want me to patch her in?"

"Yes, please," Addie said, reaching for the remote to turn on the conference room screen. "We'll also need to have Lilly and the others come back, if she is feeling up to it. Holly, I also want you on this case please."

"We are OK," they heard Nick say, and watched as Holly stepped aside to let Lilly, Nick and his mother return to the room. They immediately sat down. Lilly looked over at her father and turned her chair so that her back was to Officer Ed. Holly joined the group trying to hide her excitement.

Wolff winked at Nick and said, "Now this is where it's going to get interesting kid."

"Really," Mac replied, straightening up in his chair. "It already beats most of the cases I have worked on."

Wolff nodded in agreement, looking up as Marie's hesitant voice came through the speakers. "Hello all, can you hear me?

Wolff said, "Hey spooky lady, how ya doing?"

Maria replied, "Is that Mr. Wolff I hear?"

"You are the mind reader, you tell me?" Wolff answered laughing.

Ignoring him, Addie continued. "Marie, thank you for agreeing to talk with us. I know how you hate using the phone. Let me adjust the camera so that you can see who you are talking to. Let me introduce you to the others around the table. I assume you would like me to go clockwise, starting at my right?"

"Yes, thank you," Marie answered."

"No problem, next to me we have Laurie, who is Nick's mother. You may remember Nick from our neighborhood. I believe he read to you when you visited last."

"Yes, I remember Laurie and her wonderful pancakes, and Nick. He did read to me. Good morning."

"Is it morning down there where you are Marie? I can't believe you remember I read to you." Nick answered.

"It is morning here, about an hour later than your time. And I have a photographic memory. I can not only remember that you read to me, but I can remember what you read to me."

"Cool."

Addie continued, "Beside him we have his new friend Lilly. Next to her is Lilly's father, Mr. Louis Brisbaux. He has asked us to call him Louis. He and Lilly are our new clients. On the other side of Mr. Brisbaux we have a new associate whose specialty is forensic photography, Mr. McCoid. He goes by Mac. He is a friend of Mr. Wolff, who is sitting next to him. Across from him is our Chief of Police, Officer Edward Washington, one of our cities finest."

"Marie Levine, to those of you who have not yet had the privilege, is coming to us from the Institute of Metaphysics. She is a professor at the Institute. She has a doctorate in Theological Anthropology and Demonology as well as a master's degree in, I believe, Quantum Physics? Is that correct Marie?"

"Yes, it is," she answered very softly, as though she was making an apology. "But before we continue Addie, I believe you left someone out of your introductions."

Looking around the room, Addie confirmed that she had introduced everyone.

"No, that's everyone," Addie insisted.

"Really? Then may I begin by talking to Lilly?" Marie asked.

Addie turned the camera toward Lilly.

"Go ahead Marie," Addie instructed.

Marie said, "Lilly, do you know who I am talking about?"

"Yes," Lilly answered.

"Will you be so kind as to introduce your friend to me? She is standing next to you." Marie said, as though it was the most normal occurrence in the world.

Everyone stared Lilly, waiting to hear what she would say.

"Her name is Elizabeth," Lilly answered.

"Thank you, it's wonderful to meet you Elizabeth. Thank you for coming with Lilly today. It was nice of you to wear such a pretty dress. The flowers are lovely. Is that an apron you're wearing?"

As she asked the questions, Addie noticed Mac pulling pictures from the envelope he had brought with him. She noticed his face go pale as he flipped through them, showing them to Wolff. Wolff took a couple of the pictures from him. Mac then handed one to Louis, one to Addie, and slid one of them across the table to Ed. What they saw was a picture of a little girl wearing a dress with a flowered print. Covering the dress was a pinafore type apron that slipped over her neck and tied at the waste.

"Lilly, how did you and Elizabeth meet?" Marie asked.

"At home."

"Has she always been with you at home?"

"No, only since my mother got sick."

"Does Elizabeth ever talk to anyone else besides you?"

"Yes, she talked to my mother before she died."

"Really, did she say why she came to be with you and your mother?"

Lilly didn't answer right away. As they all watched, her face seemed to change. She looked incredibly sad. Once again Addie saw a look that she recognized. It was the same look she saw the night she had first met Lilly. Lilly's face had become transparent and it seemed as if behind the clear shell, someone else was looking out.

When Lilly spoke, they all heard the singsong voice Addie had heard the night she met Lilly. Addie realized it wasn't Lilly's voice singing, not the Lilly they knew. From the look on his face it was clear even Nick was confused by the change in his friend. All of them listened in amazement as Lilly sang.

*"Bones of mine, bones of mine,*
*I cannot rest, I will not leave,*
*Watching, waiting, till the day,*
*I find a way to make them pay."*

Lilly repeated the poem twice and then stopped. She sat there staring straight ahead.

Marie continued, "Elizabeth, I know there is a reason you have chosen Lilly, and I know you don't want to hurt her. But if you continue to communicate through her this way, you will make her weak. You will harm her health."

"No, not my Lilly. You leave my Lilly and my family alone. You're a murderer. You and your step-mother have done more damage than was ever done to you." He reached for his daughter, but Wolff stopped him, pulling him back.

"Sir," Marie's voice commanded with so much force it surprised Addie. "Please do not touch Lilly, let me handle this."

Once again in a quiet soft voice Marie confronted the young girl who now appeared to have a defiant look on her face. Nick, frightened by what he saw, had retreated from Lilly's side to his mother's, who was reassuring him that everything would be all right.

"Elizabeth," Marie continued, "You are among friends, friends that will help you to end this once and for all. I will come and help. We will find out what happened to you, and we will help you. But please, you can see that Lilly is just like you were once. She has a family who loves her and don't want her hurt. You know this is not her time. Do you understand?"

Once again the room was quiet. While they waited, Lilly answered with great sadness and anger.

"It was not my time, I could not see,
I could not answer,
Two Ponies called for me, my father cried,
It was not my time."

# CHAPTER 19

Marie said, "I know Elizabeth. I promise we will make it right. I know how to reunite you with your family. Would you like that?"

Elizabeth didn't answer, she simply left. The transparent look on Lilly's face was gone. As the group watched, the normal color came back to the young girl's face. Suddenly, Lilly slumped across the table. Wolff let go of Louis so he could scoop his daughter into his arms. Sitting down on Louis' lap, Lilly slumped against him, breathing heavily as he rocked her in his arms.

Marie asked, "Addie, tell me what you see in Lilly that I can't tell from the camera?"

Addie answered, "Lilly is back, Marie. She is exhausted. What do you want us to do next?"

"Schedule a flight for me today please. We have to take care of Elizabeth's issues as soon as possible. Elizabeth is much too strong, who knows what she'll do to Lilly. If you don't mind Addie, I would like to stay with you and Martin when I arrive. I draw so much positive energy from the two of you."

"We insist Marie. We love having you. Not to mention that the area where Elizabeth was last seen is our block, specifically the house next door."

Marie answered, "Really? Do me a favor Addie, e-mail me as much information as you have and I will read it on the plane. I look forward to seeing you all again." Before anyone could say any more they heard the click of the phone and the screen went black.

"Well, that makes it all crystal clear, "Ed said sarcastically. "What do you think this Marie will want us to do? All show up at midnight and see where the spirit leads us?" His smirk turned quickly into a frown.

"Maybe. That's up to Marie. We will let you know," Addie answered as though it was just another investigation. For a change, no one said anything.

Wolff turned to Louis and asked, "If you feel up to it, I have a few questions for you," Wolff looked down at his notebook.

"Go ahead, I will answer if I can," Louis volunteered.

"Where did you get the book?" Wolff asked.

"It has been passed down through my family. Each generation has tried to find Elizabeth, hoping that if they found her body and properly buried it, the deaths would stop. Since that day, a mother or a daughter has died in every generation before their 30th birthday."

"Explain the pattern again for me." Wolff asked.

"It is always the first wife or the first daughter" Louis answered, a bit agitated at having to repeat himself.

"So, if it has taken a mother or a daughter, what makes you think Lilly is at risk? Your wife is already dead." Wolff said bluntly.

Louis sighed. "Yes, in the past there has been only a first wife or a first daughter, but this is the first time since the day of the hanging that there has been a first daughter born to a first wife," he said as he held Lilly tightly against him. "My wife and Lilly are the first wife and first daughter."

"OK, so what connection does Elizabeth have to the house?" Wolff asked.

"I don't know for sure. From what I have been able to find out, it used to be farmland and a meadow. According to some of the notes in the book, there were some wild flowers growing there that were used for a healing tea. It was one of the places the Chief, Two Ponies and Elizabeth use to go."

"There is a story in the book, written during one of the visits to the jail that my great, great grandmother recorded. It seems the Chief made a little medicine bag and bark box for Elizabeth. When he picked flowers or herbs for his supply, he gave her some for the box and pouch. He taught her how to prepare her own medicines."

"One time, in the dead of winter, he wrote that Elizabeth's father was very ill with a fever and a horrible cough. He instructed Elizabeth to make a strong tea for her father using these flowers. She made the tea, the fever broke that night, and within days her father was strong and healthy again."

Wolff pushed his questioning further, "So if they went all along the river collecting things, I ask again, why that spot?"

Louis answered, "Because that is where Lilly feels Elizabeth. She started seeing and hearing this little girl shortly before her mother died. She never told us, but my wife and I knew there was something wrong. We thought it was the start of the grieving process. From the time of her diagnosis the doctors did not give my wife any hope. We had been told that my wife had only weeks to live. They sent her home to die."

"About a week before my wife died she started to see Elizabeth too. That is when she knew Lilly was not grieving. My wife said Elizabeth would come and stand by her bed insisting that we come here to find her. I don't expect any of you to understand, I don't understand myself. All I know is that both of them were hearing and seeing the same little girl, who was giving them the same message. So, we followed her directions and came here." He bent his head to kiss the crown of Lilly's head.

Wolff said, "OK, that's all the questions I have. So now what, Addie?"

Ed butted in, "That's what I would like to know. Does the police station need to stock up on holy water or garlic?"

"That is up to Marie, Ed. I'll let you know," Addie answered. "Until she has had a chance to evaluate the situation, we'll keep Louis and Lilly safe and away from that house. Louis, I want Tan to stay with you and Lilly. I would prefer it if Nick would bring Lilly's homework to the townhouse, if it's OK with you and Laurie? Lilly might like to have Nick stay there with the two of you in the evenings. But until Marie, Wolff and Mac have a chance to investigate further, under no circumstances are you and Lilly to go back to that house. Do you understand?"

Louis nodded. He said softly, "Yes, I will make arrangements to do my work for the city from home. We'll do whatever you say. I just want my little girl safe."

# CHAPTER 20

Nick pleaded with this mom. "Can I Mom? Can I please stay at Lilly's for a few days? I promise I will make you proud. I will eat anything her Dad cooks and I will take out his garbage..."

"That is up to Louis, Nick. If he thinks he is up to having another child around," Laurie answered.

Louis looked at Nick standing next to his mother's chair with an arm around her shoulders, the intent look of a pleading child on his face. He smiled. It was apparent that he liked this boy. But his next words surprised Addie, when he smiled at Laurie and said "You are both welcome any time."

When Addie realized that her assessment of an attraction between the two was confirmed, she thought, *Well, I'll be*.

Laurie answered, "Thank you, but I need to stay home and take care of Nick's grandpa. If you are sure that it won't be too much trouble, Nick can stay for a few nights."

Addie looked over at Wolff and could tell he was thinking the same thing she was. There were sparks in the air. Wolff rolled his eyes. Mac was grinning too when Addie looked over at him. The eye for detail these two had. If Addie had had any doubt they were the men for this job, she didn't anymore.

"Good," Addie said, grabbing the phone and pushing the button for Holly.

"What do you need Boss?" Holly asked.

"I need you to have the jet for Marie."

Holly answered, "As I recall, the last time Marie only wanted a late night flight."

Addie said, "You recall correctly. She will want to fly after midnight. She hates flying, so if she can sleep through it, she is much happier. Call Joe, Marie likes him."

"That's our Marie," Wolff chimed in.

"Great, will she be bringing her own caldron or should I line one up?" Ed asked, pushing his chair back.

"No need for that, she gets all of her supplies at the Trading Post right by Addie's," Holly answered. Without skipping a beat, she added, "I'll call Joe and let Marie know when to expect him."

"Good, it's nice to know you can always get supplies close to home," Ed said as he stood. "Well Addie, thanks again. Call me if you need me. But just so you know, I draw the line at wearing black robes and dancing around a fire at midnight," he said, smirking as Addie walked him to the door.

Before she could throw him a retort, Wolff added. "So how do you feel about snakes, Ed?"

"I hate them too," Ed answered, as he door closed behind him.

"OK, let's wrap this meeting up," Addie said.

"Mac, if you have decided to work with us, you can start your meter running."

"Wouldn't miss this for the world," Mac answered.

"OK. Wolff, before you go, take Mac down to the toy room and introduce him to the boys. Guys, do whatever you have to. I need to know that house and property inside and out."

"Hey Mac, ready to see the real Santa's workshop? Follow me."

"Right behind ya," Mac answered, stopping to shake Addie's hand, "a pleasure doing business with you, Addie."

"Thank you, Mac. I hope this is only the beginning."

Turning back to the table, Addie looked over at Louis. "Louis, I am going to take you all out to lunch while my team secures your house. Then I will drive you home, and Tan will take it from there."

"Whatever you say," Louis answered.

"Hey Addie, could I talk to you a minute in private?" Nick asked.

"Sure. If you'll excuse us, we'll be right back." Looking over at Lilly, Addie could see her strength was coming back, but she wasn't ready to leave the security of her father's lap just yet. She followed Nick out into the hall.

"OK Addie, just answer me one thing."

"If I can, Nick."

Nick tried to act as adult as he could. He said, "You think Marie can help Lilly? You saw what she did, Addie. You saw her face. For a while there, I thought for sure her head was going to start spinning and..,"

Addie interrupted. "I know, Nick. And yes, I think Marie can help Lilly. Marie is very good at what she does."

Nick asked, "What is it she does anyway?"

"That is two questions, but that's OK. I think it would be better if you waited to ask Marie yourself. I will tell you this much, she can see and talk to Elizabeth just like I'm talking to you right now."

"No duh Addie, I could see that. But can she make Elizabeth stop? Can she make her go away and leave Lilly alone?"

"That depends on a lot of things and it can get very complicated. Do you remember two years ago when I was gone for a month?" Addie asked.

"Like I could forget, I thought Martin was going to have some kind of breakdown. It was sick. I kept trying to tell him, man she is only a girl, get over it."

"Yes, I am only a girl. Just like Lilly is only a girl, right?" Addie said reaching out to tousle his hair.

"Cut it out Addie. You are not going to throw me off the track that easy. What is your going away got to do with this thing anyway?"

"When I was gone, I was at the college where Marie teaches. I spent a month working with her and some of our other operatives on a very special case in New Orleans. If I didn't believe she was the one for this job, I wouldn't have called her. Let's just say one of her specialties is finding missing children."

"Yeah, but this isn't like your ordinary missing kid. Not only is she dead, she is way dead and way mean."

"Don't worry about Marie. Believe me, I've seen her handle some of the meanest. Besides, I am not so sure Elizabeth is mean as much as she is angry about something that happened to her. When we hurt, sometimes we hurt others."

"Yeah, well you know we are counting on you, Addie."

"I know Nick, and I won't let you down," Addie said, putting her arms around him, pulling him close. She felt her eyes water while Nick hugged her back, hard.

— — — —

The airport was dead at three am. *The witching hour,* Addie thought while she waited for Marie. Before the plane came into sight, Addie felt her. Standing, she adjusted the paper wrapped around the roses Martin had bought for Marie. She had only been standing a few seconds when she saw the plane come around the side of the hanger and stop in front. As Marie came walking slowly toward her, Addie saw the slight limp that only a few people would notice.

It took her back, remembering how it happened. She had been there with Marie and another medium, working a seriously difficult case in New Orleans. The presiding medium had succeeded in making contact with an entity that decided to play rough. Before Addie could pull her out of the way, a brick flew across the warehouse. It struck Marie, knocking her to the ground. Addie rushed to help her up, but not fast enough. As they tried to scramble out of the way, a heavy crate came crashing down on Marie's leg, breaking it. Marie still had a slight limp when she was tired.

"Are you OK? Would you like me to pull the car up?" Addie asked as she hugged her friend.

"Don't be silly. Are those for me?" Marie asked reaching for the flowers, pressing them to her nose.

"Who else? It's not like Martin would let one of his favorite girls go without flowers."

"You know, he did this to make me feel guilty for taking you away from him for a month."

"Probably. Let's get you to our place. You are going to need all the rest you can get. Joe will bring the bags."

"You mean bag. She only has one," Joe said, walking behind them.

"God, it's good to know you never change," Addie said, directing her to the car. All the way home Marie filled her in on her latest field of study. When Addie was done asking questions, Marie had a few of her own.

"Now for the case at hand, what does your heart tell you Addie? Tell me your impressions of this little girl."

"Which little girl, the live one or the dearly departed?"

"You know me, let's start with the departed first."

"I think she is very sad, and very angry. I think she was killed in a violent way. She wants to be found and she wants someone to pay. I think she wants to be back with her family, but has no idea how to reach them and that makes the anger worse."

"Good, we are on the same page. I meditated on the plane. I am not sure about her yet. It would help if I had something of hers to touch, but I keep seeing the same pictures in my head."

"What pictures Marie?" Addie asked, trying to listen and keep her mind on her driving. Thank God the traffic was light this time of the night.

"Are you sure you want to know?"

"No, but I need to."

"All right, but once I do, I can't take it back. You know that."

"Yes, go ahead."

Marie said, "I believe Elizabeth suffered greatly before her body died."

"You mean like torture?"

"In a fashion" Marie said, reaching across to lay a hand on Addie's arm.

"What do you mean...?" Before the words were even out of her mouth, Addie saw what Marie meant. "Oh my God," Addie said and felt the car swerve. Marie immediately removed her hand from Addie's arm, and Addie regained control of the car.

Marie said, "I'm sorry. I should know not to do that while you are driving."

In control now, Addie turned to look over at Marie. "That can't be right, that can't be the way it happened. I cannot believe that any of the town's people would have done that to a little girl."

Sighing, Marie looked over at Addie, wishing she'd waited to tell her. "Don't you see Addie? She wasn't just a little girl. She was a little girl who had befriended a wanted Native American Chief. There has to be more to the story than we know yet. There are pieces missing like who are the other two men and the woman that I keep seeing in flashes. They are all involved somehow, and it all seems to revolve around some information they thought Elizabeth had. The other thing we know is they would stop at nothing to find out, even if it meant murdering a little girl."

# CHAPTER 21

Wolff was waiting for Addie and Marie when they pulled into the driveway of Addie's home. From one of the benches near the patio, he stood and waved at Addie and Marie.

"Good early morning Ladies. Still traveling in the dead of night I see," he said while strolling across the driveway to open Marie's door, and to offer her his hand.

"Thank you, Mr. Wolff. Up early yourself, I see."

"The early bird catches the worm. Isn't that what they say?"

"I believe so, but don't tell me you are looking for worms?"

"No. As a matter of fact, I am looking to catch something much more elusive."

"And that would be?" She asked, walking over to Addie's yard swing, sitting down. She began to swing slowly back and forth. From here she had a full view of the house and yard next door.

"A little girl," he answered, noticing that Marie was staring right past him at the yard. He walked over and stood next to her, trying to see what she was looking at.

"What is it, Marie? Do you see something?" Addie asked, returning from the garage and handing Wolff Marie's carpetbag.

She lifted her hand and pointed to the old oak tree. Wolff and Addie followed the direction of her finger, trying to see what she saw.

"Addie do you see anything?" Wolff asked.

"No, but what counts is what Marie is seeing."

"What is it you see Marie?" Addie asked.

"I see Elizabeth sitting next to the base of that old oak tree, she is leaning against it. She is writing in a book and has

130

something lying next to her on the ground. Elizabeth is closing the book now and gathering up what was on the ground. It must be heavy, she seems to be struggling a little. She has gone behind the tree now."

Without saying another word, Marie stood and walked toward the back door of Addie's house, Addie following close behind. Turning, Marie looked back over her shoulder at Wolff who was still standing next to the swing, looking at the tree.

"You see Mr. Wolff, finding your worms will be much harder than finding our Elizabeth. Now if you don't mind, I would like to rest for a while. I am not as young as the two of you." Marie said, walking into the house.

Wolff followed them in.

"When Mac gets here, we are going to take a real close look at that tree. Addie should I take Marie's bag to the guest room upstairs?" he asked.

"No, the one at the end of the study is where I sleep. All those steps are too much for my knee these days," Marie said.

When Wolff returned he bent down to give Marie a kiss on the forehead, before he crossed the kitchen and headed for the door. "Man that is some Hoodoo you do Marie."

"Thank you, I think," Marie answered, smiling over at Addie who was heating water for tea.

When he was out of earshot Marie said, "I think that poor boy is hanging around with the wrong kind of women Addie," Marie accepted the cup of chamomile tea Addie handed her in an ornate porcelain cup.

"I think you may be right about that Marie," pouring herself some and sitting down on the opposite side of the table.

"You are a lot like her, you know," Marie said, setting her cup back in the saucer.

"A lot like who? Addie asked "Elizabeth?"

"No silly, your grandma Clara. These are some of her cups right?"

"Yes, but how did you know…"

Marie smiled back and took another sip.

— — — —

Wolff had left the ladies, but not the property. He walked over to the little house and all around the yard. There was no sign of any snakes. He walked over to the old oak tree and there in the spot where Marie had described seeing Elizabeth was a slight indentation in the grass, like someone had been sitting in that spot. *I'll be damned, kid. What are you up to?* He looked down at his watch it was almost 5:00 a.m. *The sun should be coming up any minute*, he thought. Then he sat down in the exact place of the indentation. When he did, a chill ran up his back, but the place he was sitting was warm.

"I'm going to sit here Elizabeth, in your spot. If you want, we can be friends. Or not, suit yourself, but this is my spot now." He said aloud.

He waited, but nothing happened. He leaned back against the tree and fell asleep, but it was far from a restful sleep. He dreamed that he saw a book. It was big when it was opened. He moved in for a closer look and realized that it was a ledger book, the kind that accountants used. He couldn't make out the entries, and then the book slammed shut just as he grabbed for it. When he lifted it, blood ran out from the bottom of the book.

The next thing he knew, he was running with the book. It was so heavy. Then everything was dark. There were trees all around him and a strong smell. What was it? The river. It was the same smell that he experienced every time he walked or rode his bike along the trails behind Addie's house. He was in the woods behind Addie's house and he knew it.

Then he saw the tree that had the big hollow spot, and he knew that tree. He stopped at the tree, put the book inside, and covered it with leaves and branches. He had the feeling that there was someone with him, but he didn't know who. He didn't fear this person. It felt more like when Addie and him were on a case and were canvassing an area. You know your partner is there at your back. That was how it felt, like he had a partner in this. Then everything went black. He woke up with a start when he heard Mac calling.

"Morning Wolff, have you been here all night?" Mac called as he got out of his car, cradling the camera he had gotten from the toyshop yesterday.

"It sure seems like it." He said, standing and feeling like he had run over a mile. He couldn't believe that he'd fallen asleep on the job. Not to mention out in the open.

"Wolff, were you sleeping by that old tree when I drove up? I haven't known you to sleep much ever, out in the open like that. Is something going on that you should talk to your partner about?" Mac asked with concern.

"Man, what time is it?" Wolff asked Mac.

"7:00 a.m. So how long were you sitting there?"

"The last thing I remember was looking at my watch and it was around 5:30 a.m. I told Elizabeth that I was going to take her spot. I wasn't tired, but I fell asleep and the dream I had … I remember everything and I need to write it down. Do you mind giving me a minute?"

"No man, go ahead. I can't wait to hear about this. Tell me where you want me to start taking pictures while I still have this light, and I will leave you alone."

Wolff pointed to the tree he had been sitting at. "The tree and the house Mac, I want pictures of all over that tree. As soon as I write my notes, I am going to get a ladder so that I can climb up and see if there is anything odd about the

133

Y in the tree. This tree is connected to Elizabeth somehow, and I am going to find out how."

"OK, so besides that, is anything else going on this morning that I should know about?"

"Oh, not much. I've just been hanging around with two ladies, swinging over there in Addie's yard. Of course while Addie and I were just being normal, Marie was watching Elizabeth around that tree over there. On a lighter note, I guess the better half was alright with you working with us. You are here early, all bright eyed and ready to go." He said pulling out his notebook starting to write.

"Sure she is, as long as I don't miss our weekly card game, that's where she draws the line. Now what is this about swinging and seeing ghosts in trees?"

"When Addie brought Marie home from the airport, Marie sat down in Addie's swing before going into the house. I guess she must have felt or saw Elizabeth as they were driving in. Anyway, she saw her sitting below the tree and watched her as she got up and walked behind it. She had something with her, a book for sure, and something else that Marie could not make out. I just want to make sure that we take a close look at that tree."

"No problem," Mac answered, turning toward the property and starting to shoot the tree from a distance. Wolff finished writing, closed his book, and slipped it into his jacket pocket. That's when an urge hit him. It was so strong that he was half way to the garage before Mac noticed what he was doing.

"Hey Wolff, where you going? The tree is over here."

"I have to get one of Martins ladders." Wolff called back.

"Ladder what for?"

"I don't know. I just have to get a ladder."

Mac stood there watching as Wolff went into the garage and emerged with an expandable ladder. *What on earth was going on around here? Wolff falling asleep next to a tree dreaming, and now a compulsion to get a ladder, what next?* He wondered.

"Hey, wait up Wolff. Boy, are you growly as all get-out this morning. You're right about those guys in Addie's shop. I can't believe they had one these old things," Mac said as he held up a Paraktica EE3 camera in mint condition. "Digital cameras now days just can't do every job in my opinion. Not to mention you can alter everything with them. I prefer the oldies. And finding one of these, much less being able to use it, is a dream come true."

"That is what I am counting on Mac," Wolff said, standing next to the tree and holding a ladder. "God, I want this job over with. I am starting to doubt everything I have ever believed."

Mac chuckled a bit and said, "Don't get too fired up until we have a look around. Marie or no Marie, she will have to show me something that I can sink my teeth into before she has me believing in ghostly girls."

Wolff shrugged. "I thought the same thing until two years ago when I was on assignment with Addie in New Orleans. It was right after Addie hired me. I was tasked with nothing but keeping the ladies safe and I couldn't do it. You can't fight against something you can't see."

Mac's eyes narrowed. He said, "You've never talked about that assignment Wolff. Just like you never talked much about your time in the NSA. What happened in New Orleans?"

"You wouldn't believe me even if I did tell you. But I will tell you this much, my job was to protect Addie and Marie. What I was fighting against, as Marie calls them, were demonic spirits. But that wasn't the only enemy around.

There were also some very dangerous men, the living kind. Before Addie was called in to help, they had killed two of the founders of the firm. Addie was in a rage and insisted on handling it on her own. She had always been tight with one of the old guys. She had worked for him in the Navy. But her partner Ellis wouldn't let her go alone. He told me that he thought whoever was killing off the old guys was out to get everyone in the firm."

"Was he right?"

Wolff nodded. "It was one of those inner circle things. It only takes one on the inside who turns, and mayhem follows. He was the one man everyone trusted. The investigation led to an old warehouse along the river front in New Orleans. It was me, Addie, Marie and a local Medium. They were supposed to wait in the car. I would do the walk and secure the parameter and then come back for them when it was safe. We would do a walk around to see what we could find, and then leave. I was half way around my walk when I heard Addie and Marie scream into my ear piece."

"They went in the warehouse without you?"

"Marie said later that she goes where the spirit leads. And when it leads her, she is in the zone. There is no stopping her, and Addie had to follow. Addie didn't think to give me the heads up until they were in an all-out battle with God knows what. But I tell you as sure as I am standing here, I don't ever want to see or hear what I did that night. I still have nightmares. And you know I have seen more than my share of combat, not to mention all the tight spots I have been in since. Mac, I can dish it out and I can take it. But when you can't see or feel your enemy until it hits you and you don't know how or what it's going to hit you with, that is a whole different ball game. Now remember, if you tell anyone this, I will have to kill you." Wolff said without smiling.

Mac laughed. "Well if you do end up killing me, then you'll have to worry about what I might throw at you from beyond. We had better get to work. After all, that's what the ladies are paying for. What do you want me to do?" Mac asked as he began adjusting the camera.

Wolff said, "Do what you do best, just keep taking pictures. Capture the entire tree, especially right here. Let me know when I can climb up and have a look."

Mac aimed his camera and began shooting. Wolff stood back watching until Mac motioned to him. As soon as Mac did, Wolff positioned the ladder against the tree. He started climbing up in the general area where Marie had seen Elizabeth.

Wolff uttered, "Well I'll be damned."

"What is it?" Mac called up, "What did you find?"

"Do you think you can climb up here and take some pictures?"

"Sure, I may be retired but I'm not a cripple."

Wolff climbed down and held the ladder, surprised at how easily his old friend scampered up the rungs.

Mac shouted down, "Looks like this old tree has a hollow spot right here at the Y where it braches off. You can't see it from the ground, but once you get up here its plain as day. The hollow maybe deeper than you would think."

Mac angled the camera and clicked away. Then he grabbed a digital camera from his pocket and climbed up as far as he could. He positioned the camera in the hole and took a couple of shots. Suddenly, there was a look of surprise on his face.

"Hey Wolff, it looks like there maybe something in here, but it is down to far for me to get a hold of it."

"Come on down. I will climb up and see if I can reach it," Wolff called.

The men exchanged places. Mac watched as Wolff's arm disappeared into the hole. Wolff started cussing and then struggled with pulling at something. It sounded like the insides of the tree were being ripped apart. Wolff started back down the ladder and was holding a very dirty metal box. It was partially wrapped in shreds of burlap.

Wolff walked over to the old picnic table. He laid the box down and stepped back, letting Mac get some close up shots.

In the background they heard Martin yell to them. "Hey, what do you boys got there? Pretty early to be climbing trees isn't it?" Martin was crossing the yard, carrying a mug of hot coffee in each hand.

# CHAPTER 22

"Where did you get that box?" Martin asked, handing them each a cup of coffee.

Wolff answered as he pointed to the scrapes on his arms, "Stuck tight in that old oak. It looked like the tree started to grow around it some. I had a hell of a time getting it out."

"That is quite a lock on it. Are you going to open it?" Martin asked.

"Yeah, you got any ideas? Maybe a crow bar or your cutting torch?"

"I think I can find something," Martin said, as he turned to walk back toward the garage.

He had only taken a few steps when he heard the sound of metal sliding on metal behind him. Turning around he saw the two men staring intensely at the box on the picnic table. The color had drained from both of their faces. Martin raced back. As soon as he reached them, he noticed the lock was opened.

Martin asked, "How did you guys get that lock open?"

Neither one answered right away.

Finally Mac said, "We didn't. I swear by all that is holy, it just made a sound like someone slid a key in the lock and turned it, and then the box opened itself. What the hell is going on here, Wolff?"

"Well, if I had to guess I would say that the ghost girl is back," Martin answered. "Or maybe the lock wasn't really locked tight. And with all that pulling, you loosened it."

"I think you were right the first time. It's Elizabeth," Wolff answered.

Martin shrugged. "Even though I am married to Addie, it took me a while to get used to spirits. But, after a while..."

Mac asked, "After a while? You mean things like this happen a lot around here?"

Martin answered, "Not a lot, but there are times. And actually, once is more than enough to change your attitude."

Wolff cut him off. "I don't care how this box opened or who opened it. Right now, I just want to see what is inside of it. Who wants the honors? I don't want to be accused of having all the fun."

"No way am I doing it, "Mac answered, standing back from the table. "This is your case you are the boss. I am just here to take pictures."

"Ah, I am goanna be late for work," Martin said while walking backwards toward his truck. "See you guys here or in the hereafter." Martin turned and headed to his pickup. He could wait until later to hear what was inside the box. Addie would tell him everything.

"Smart asses. Guess that only leaves me," Wolff said, bending over the box as he tugged at the lid.

Surprisingly, the contents were fairly dry. Then again, the lid had been shut tight. In the box was a carved wooden doll, not much bigger than Wolff's hand. It was dressed in a simple dress, with a faded blue flowered print and a belt of twine around her waist. There was also a pouch, most likely deerskin, with beaded work on the front. Instead of a draw-string, it had a flap that was held shut by a piece of bone or tooth. There were two other small toys. At the bottom of the box, wrapped in the same animal skin and tied up with a piece of twine, was a bundle that could be a book.

He picked up the bundle and was about to unwrap it when the sharpness of Marie's voice stopped him in his tracks.

"Mr. Wolff, give me that. Do not open it," she yelled, as she and Addie walked slowly across the yard.

He hadn't heard that tone since he had been a boy in private school. He stopped and waited for the women to make their way. As he watched Marie, the thought occurred to him that she seemed a little slower than when they had last worked together. Yet, the rest of her never seemed to age. *How old was she was anyway?* He wondered.

He was snapped out of his thoughts when he felt Marie tug at the bundle. He looked her in the eye and saw what looked like understanding, or possibly just a knowing look. He realized that she knew what he was thinking. He was at a loss for words. This whole thing was just too much. He felt Mac leaning closer to him.

Mac whispered, "How did she know to come out here just now? How did she know that we'd found something?

Mac shouldn't have bothered to lower his voice. Marie knew what he was saying. She said, "I was resting, until Elizabeth woke me."

With Addie standing quietly beside her, Marie picked up the bundled items.

She instructed, "Addie, I need a white candle and some of that dried sage you keep."

"What the Sam hell is she planning to do?" Mac asked, stepping even closer to Wolff.

"I don't have a clue. But if this is anything like the last time, pull on your big boy boots Mac, it could be a wild ride," Wolff answered. As they walked back to the house with Addie and Marie, Mac nodded, adjusting the camera for inside shots.

Once inside, Marie cleared the kitchen table. She went to the guest room and returned with a small black bag. From it she removed a very old, beat up looking metal candleholder, a metal dish that looked like it had been around since the dark ages and had obviously been used to burn things in, and a small black book. As the two men watched in silence,

Addie placed a white candle in the holder. She then lay what looked like a small bundle of dried plants in the bowl, along with a couple of large farmers wooden matches. Next to the dish she laid a large feather painted with, of all things, the head of a wolf.

Mac poked Wolff with an elbow as if to say, did you see that? Wolff didn't respond.

Frustrated, Mac said, "See that wolf on the feather? This is getting weird."

Wolff answered, "What do you mean getting?"

Marie looked over to Mac and asked, "Mr. Mac is it?"

"Ah, yes ma'am. My name is McCoid, but everyone calls me Mac."

Marie said, holding out a pen to him. "I'll need you and Mr. Wolff to write your full legal names down on this piece of paper. Please include your middle name and any name you received from your church."

"Why?" Mac asked, as he bent over the paper and added his name below that of Addie and Marie.

"Addie will explain as we go along," Marie answered. Taking the paper from Mac, she passed it to Wolff. When he handed it back she looked at the names and folded the paper in what looked like a triangle shape, tucking in the corners. She placed the paper in the palm of her left hand, then covered it over with her right and mumbled a prayer of some kind. Then she placed the folded paper in the metal bowl.

Marie nodded at Addie who lit the candle and the small bundle of sage, before dropping it in the bowl. Marie waited as Addie picked up the feather and walked all around the room sweeping the feather across the smoldering bundle, chanting under her breath. Addie then returned the small bowl and feather to the table, and allowed the bundle to smolder like incense.

She sat down at the table, and Marie opened the black book. They all watched intently as Marie began reciting something about consecrating warriors and rocking back and forth. Mac stepped over to Addie. Wolff heard him ask if he should be taking pictures. Addie nodded, and Mac started snapping pictures.

Finally, Marie stopped chanting and sat down, quietly rocking back and forth. She appeared to be completely unaware of their presence. Addie stood up and walked over to the two men. She could tell that an explanation was due. Stepping close but keeping her voice low, she started to explain.

Addie said, "Marie is with us in body, but not necessarily in soul. She is completing a prayer for protection and strength for the names on the paper."

"Protection and strength? I can protect us." Wolff told her. "I don't need prayers."

Addie reminded him, "Really, just like last time? You need them more than you think." Addie answered.

Mac said, "Wolff, I think we are way out of our element here. This is Marie's turf. The way I see it, a little praying can't hurt."

"Fine, let her pray. Addie what were you doing?"

"The bundle in the bowl is sage and it is used to cleanse the air of evil." She explained.

As the three watched Marie, suddenly a burst of cold air shot through the kitchen window. The candle blew out, and Addie immediately picked up a match and rushed to relight it. Her eyes scanned the room and addressed Elizabeth, as though she were her own child.

Addie said, "Elizabeth, stop that. You're not impressing anyone, I am sure your mother taught you better manners than that."

The room turned colder. It was a cold that made them all shiver. Then the candle blew out once again.

Addie demanded, "Elizabeth, this is a house of peace. We have been good neighbors to you and will continue to be. In return, I demand that you be respectful of my house."

The breeze ceased and gradually the room grew warm again.

"Thank you Elizabeth," Addie said.

As the two men stood there with Wolff in a ready watchful position, the door to the patio slowly slid open. The smell that assaulted their noses was putridly sour and had the sharp edge of sulfur.

"What the hell?" Wolff shouted.

Marie's body stiffened. She turned to her left, addressing someone only she could see. With a very stern and determined voice she made it clear that she knew she was in the presence of a woman and could see her.

Marie then told her that she must be civil and state her business or she would be banished. Marie continued on as though all the others could hear and see what she could.

"Tell me your name and who you are. You are compelled by our Lord Jesus to do so." Then she stopped as though she was listening. As they watched, Marie smiled knowingly.

"Addie, what is she doing?" Wolff asked.

"Having a conversation with someone," Addie answered and reached for his arm to secure his attention. "Watch and learn."

"Madame, I assure you that we are not fools and neither was your stepdaughter or her friend Two Ponies. You accomplished nothing but destroying yourself and all those who were your accomplices. I can only hope that they found peace before they passed over. I know the Chief did."

The air in the room grew ice cold all around the small group, and the smell intensified. A heavy glass vase on the windowsill flew at Marie. Wolff blocked it while Addie caught it before it hit the stone floor.

"Silence yourself woman. There is a hedge of protection around this house, and all that are here, including Elizabeth. You are not in control here, I am! I will find out why you are here and I will break the hold you have on Elizabeth, her family, and this town. Before I am done, you will be bound until the judgment day when you can answer for what you have done to him who has the right to judge."

As Marie continued to pray, the smell increased. A wind whipped through the kitchen, blowing papers off the table and blowing out the candle. This time, Addie didn't bother to relight it. Addie reached out to touch Marie's shoulder and then reached for Wolff's hand, while indicating to Wolff that he take Mac's. Addie said, "Mac, complete the circle and touch Marie's other shoulder."

He did as he was told while Marie continued, this time in words that none of them understood. The whole room seemed to sway and move, making them all dizzy and nauseous.

Marie declared, "You are done. You must leave and not ever enter this house again. Go where you wish for now, but never enter this house again!" As soon as Marie had finished speaking, the spinning of the room ended and the wind died down. But before the last of the smell left, they all heard a woman's voice loud and clear before it faded.

It said, "Die!"

Immediately following the voice they heard heavy footsteps walk across the stone floor toward the door, the smell trailing after it, along with the cold air in the room. Each of them found themselves gasping to catch their breaths, all except Marie that is. Calmly, she looked to her side and said, "You can come out now Elizabeth. Your stepmother is gone."

A different smell filled the air and a cool but soft breeze moved around each one of them.

Marie said, "Don't worry Elizabeth; we are all fine and so are you. You see this hedge I have put around you is like a cloak. You can come and go and even reach out and touch us, but your stepmother cannot get to you. As long as you do what the Chief taught you, hold on to love and joy, not hatred or revenge."

"Your friends have gone on because they had no unfinished business. They wanted you to come too, but you were determined to have revenge. So not only are you still here, but you have held your stepmother's soul here too. Instead of hurting her, you have made her stronger. We'll help you end this if you cooperate. The Chief and Two Ponies are waiting for you."

As she spoke, the scent in the room changed again, this time to an overwhelming scent of flowers.

Wolff asked, "Mac, do you smell that?"

Mac answered, "Flowers, yeah I do. And did you notice…?"

"What?" Wolff asked.

"There are no flowering plants in the kitchen." Mac informed him.

Wolff began, "That's because…"

"I'm allergic," Addie interjected. "Have a seat. Marie's ready to look at the bundle."

# CHAPTER 23

Louis walked softly past his daughter's room, down the hall of his townhouse to the stairs. The smell brought back memories of wonderful breakfasts that he'd shared with his wife and Lilly. When he entered the dining area, he was surprised by what he saw on the other side of the serving bar. Nick was hard at work at the stove and the bodyguard Addie had assigned to them, Tan, was rinsing a plate at the sink.

"That smells wonderful Nick. What are you cooking," Louis asked.

"French toast, cause you're French. Where's Lilly? I will make some for her." Nick answered.

Louis said, "I think we should let her sleep. Are you all ready for school? I'll drop you off and then pick up your mom. She is going to watch Lilly today while I check on the site."

"Cool," Nick said, sliding a plate to Louis who was seated on the other side of the counter.

Tan interrupted. "Not cool. I'll call her and cancel. " He walked straight past Louis to the living room. He was out of site before Louis could object.

"I thought he would say that," Nick said, "but hey, happy Friday the 13th. It's a lucky day for everyone."

"Happy Friday the 13th?" Louis asked, looking over the bar at his young friend who was flooding his toast in syrup. I didn't know you Americans thought it was lucky?"

"I didn't use to, untill Addie and Martin moved in." Nick answered. "Milk or OJ?"

"Coffee, if you made some," Louis said, biting into his first bite of French toast.

"Sure did. And, if you don't mind, I think I will have some too, along with my milk," Nick added quickly.

Louis said, "Of course I don't mind. I was drinking Café au Lait when I was much younger than you. That's French for coffee and milk. My mother made it with a little strong coffee in the bottom of a cup, topped with steamed milk. Sometimes, she added cinnamon or coco to the top."

"For real?" Nick asked.

"For real. You were telling me how Addie and Martin made you see Friday the 13th as a good day?" Louis asked.

"Oh, yeah. See, Addie and Martin met on Friday the 13th and they were married on some kind of Jewish special day that just happened to fall on April 13th of that year. Something about two bad sticks being thrown into some bad water way back in the old days and God turned the water from bitter to sweet. Addie says that is just like her and Martin."

"How so?"

"Cause they both had some bad times in the past. Martin had just moved back to Minnesota from Iowa to help out his mom, and started up a business here. They call his mom Punky. I don't know why, but it's cool. Anyway, the bosses at Addie's work hired him to build Addie's apartment. You should ask to see it. Man it has all kinds of neat stuff. Addie was away on business and when she got back Martin showed her around it, since she would be living there. I don't know about the women in your life Louis, but it's been my experience if you show a woman a button, they just have to push it. From what I understand in Addie's apartment, you could blow something up if you press the wrong button, so Martin was there to tell her how everything worked. Well it was Friday the 13th and Martin says it was love at first sight. And four months later, they got married. Can you believe that?"

"I see what you mean, that would make it a good day for me too," Louis agreed.

Nick's faced turned serious and he asked, "Do you miss your wife?"

Louis answered, "More with each passing day. It seems like the older Lilly gets, the more she reminds me of her mother. Finish your breakfast, Nick. Your mother would be very unhappy with me if you don't eat a good breakfast." Louis stood up and walked to the door. He opened it and looked surprised when nothing was there.

"Your newspaper is on the table." Tan said from behind him, making Louis jump.

"*Mon Duire*, I didn't even hear you behind me."

"Good," Tan answered. "Remember, I said to stay away from the doors and windows. I have arranged for someone to pick up Nick's schoolwork and bring it to him. He's staying here today."

"Tan, why all the security?" Louis asked, grabbing the paper from the table, following Tan toward the living room.

"It's simple, Mr. Brisbaux," Tan answered turning to face him. "We have no idea what's going on and until we do, we assume the worst and we secure everything." Without waiting for Louis to ask any more questions, Tan simply turned and walked away.

Louis just stood there for a minute not knowing if he should be mad or happy that Addie's people seemed to think of everything.

"Hey Mr. Brisbaux, are you OK? Can I warm up your coffee?" Nick said, reaching for his cup.

"Thanks Nick. I was just thinking, maybe your mom and grandpa would like to have dinner with us here tonight. Would you like that?"

"Sure, I think they would too. Grandpa eats anything as long as there is plenty of it. That is if you and Lilly are up to his stories."

"I think we can handle them, unless they are ghost stories."

"Nope, Grandpa doesn't believe in any after life."

"Good, I'll talk to Mr. Tan and see if we can arrange it," Louis sighed.

— — — —

"OK, let's run down what we know," Wolff said, standing and pacing around Addie's kitchen table while Addie, Marie, and Mac sat patiently. "From the book Louis has, and Elizabeth's notes in the book that we found in the tree, we know that Elizabeth trusted the Chief and Two Ponies. They seemed to be the only ones she trusted."

"I agree," Addie said. "It sounded like she spent every moment she could with Two Ponies and his family. There may well have been a budding romance between the two."

"I think you are right." Mac said. "They took long walks together and her journal also says that Two Ponies made the toys we found in the box for her as a birthday gift."

Wolff added, "But she did feel like she was being followed by someone that she didn't trust."

Addie added, "Elizabeth writes that the last few days before she disappeared, she was sure of that. She actually identified several men, three of whom she saw repeatedly."

"Elizabeth was one smart little cookie," Wolff added.

"You said it, Mr. Wolff. Who knows what great things this little girl could have done for mankind had she lived." Marie added.

"Elizabeth also wrote that she had asked Two Ponies to meet her in the woods at place they both knew. She wanted to show him something. She asked him to meet her around midnight. She writes they should use what the Chief taught them to throw the watchers off their trail. That's what she called the men who were following her, the watchers. Tell me, what are you thinking Addie?" Marie asked looking over at her friend.

Addie answered, "I was thinking that the watchers were determined to be the ones who found the Chief in order to bring him back. Whether they were after a monetary reward or it just the notoriety, it's hard to tell. With the trail getting colder by the day, their agitation level would have been rising. They needed information fast and thought Elizabeth was their best bet, maybe their only one, but she wasn't talking."

Mac added, "Why do you think they wanted the chief so bad? I know Native Americans were always wanted, but it almost sounds like it was more than that. It sounds like the grandson had something and hid it. Didn't Louis's story talk about a big book that Elizabeth brought to show Two Ponies one night?"

"Yes and so does this journal." Marie added, thumbing through the book until she came to the place she was searching for. "Just listen to Elizabeth's words. 'I found the book I heard them talking about. I'm going to hide it until I can show it to father. Once he sees this, he'll believe me and I hope he'll send her away forever. She hates me and I know she is trying to kill me. I can't eat at home anymore because every time I do, I get sick. Her friends think I don't see them, but there is always one of them watching me.' That was the last entry in the journal," Marie said closing the old book.

"The book she is talking about, last night I had a dream about a book." Wolff said, pulling out his note book where he recounted the dream. "The book she found, what could it have had in it that would convince her father to send her stepmother away? It would have to be really bad if the stepmother is still hanging around trying to shut both her and us up. I mean, it's been almost two hundred years, hasn't it?" Wolff added.

Addie said, "I have no idea what it could be. But, it was the time of the Sioux uprising and the subsequent hangings in Mankato. I always thought that was the reason the Chief fled to Canada, but maybe not. My guess is, the watchers got tired of watching and grabbed her, to try and scare her."

"But from what Marie read, I don't think Elizabeth knew where the Chief was. She only knew that he left and would get a message to her. Or that he would come back when he could. A few days ago, Marie had a vision of what happened to Elizabeth at the hands of the watchers. I pray that she is wrong, but she hardly ever is."

All eyes turned to Marie. She wrapped the old book up like it had been. She mumbled a few words that were too soft for anyone else to hear. She looked up and said, "The rest of the story is for Elizabeth to tell, but she will only tell us through Lilly. We need to talk to Lilly and her father. Together, they will need to decide if they are willing to continue."

Mac asked, "This is all new to me, but can't you do it? Can't you let Elizabeth talk through you?"

"Yes Sir, I have been a channel many times. Elizabeth can talk through me if she chooses to. I have offered her my voice, but she declined. She wants her voice to be, how can I say it, closer to who she is. She wants to speak for herself, tell her story, and Lilly is her age. She is very angry at the way the watchers tried to get her to say things, they controlled her and it was adults that killed her. It's like she wants no part of us. Adults were not supposed to act like they did. They weren't supposed to hurt her. They were supposed to be there to protect her. And then there is the woman who betrayed her, her own stepmother. I'm sure that's the reason she doesn't want to speak through me. She doesn't trust any adult."

"Unfortunately, I understand what she means by not trusting," Mac answered, the look on his face telling everyone he had seen children hurt before.

Addie stated firmly, "I will talk to Louis and Lilly. Marie, do you have a feeling for where you want to have the meeting if they agree, and when?"

Marie answered, "In the house next door, as soon as it can be arranged. Addie, did you notice how adamant Elizabeth's stepmother was when she said that she owned this town? If you can spare Holly, we need her to work her magic and get us any information she can about Elizabeth's stepmother." Marie answered.

Addie said, "No problem, Wolff and Holly can do it together."

Wolff sputtered, "Help Holly? First you give me a boy as a partner and now you want me to team up with a receptionist? Seriously Addie!"

Addie responded, "Yes seriously, Wolff. For your information, Holly is my Executive Manager of Operations, not a receptionist. I'm surprised at you. I never expected you to judge a book by its cover. You are slipping back into the dark ages."

Wolff asked, "Slipping? That'll be the day, Addie. Just what is it that you think I am missing when it comes to Holly?"

Addie responded, "OK big man, just remember you asked. First of all, my young and I might add beautiful Executive Manager would love to play tame the Wolff man. Second, she has a master's degree in forensic surveillance, with a specialty in information analysis. I stole her away from the FBI because she likes to work from home sometimes. Should I go on?"

Wolff answered, "Tame the Wolff man? Really, Addie? And no you don't need to continue, I get the picture."

Mac interjected, "I think we all do. Man, how could you miss that young woman was on your trail? Even I picked up on that. Do you and I need to have a talk or something?"

Wolff said, "No, old man. I know all I need to know where the ladies are concerned. Besides, we all have work to do. Addie, so where do we find Holly this morning?" He said as he and Mac headed for the door.

"You are the great investigator, you tell me." Addie said, watching the men leave.

As soon as they had driven off, Addie called Holly at home.

Addie said, "Hey girl, don't bother coming in today. Wolff and Mac are on the way over. I want you to dazzle them with how you can look up information. If you're not wearing something like that salmon pink robe I brought back for you from Paris, I suggest you are when they get there."

Holly laughed and asked, "Addie, have you lost your mind? Are you drunk or something?"

"Nope, just playing cupid while letting you work from home in your PJ's. One other thing, take this information down. I need you to set up a meeting."

"Go ahead and start talking. My computer has voice recognition software, remember. Tell it what you need and I will arrange it. I can listen to it when I get out of the shower. By then, I will be having coffee in my slinky robe."

"Atta girl. Have fun making our Wolff drool."

# CHAPTER 24

Over the phone, Addie finished dictating the meeting instructions for Holly and hung up. It was high time she asked Holly to be more involved in the firm's caseload as an operative. Ever since the New Orleans job, Holly had begged to see Marie work. Holly was fascinated by the New Orleans case. She had labeled it Pirate's Alley when she worked on the file.

If everything worked out right today, Addie knew Holly might get her chance to see Marie in action as early as tonight. But right now, both she and Marie needed to recharge. It was bound to be a long day and night. Addie walked back and joined Marie, who was still sitting at the kitchen table.

As soon as Addie said down, Marie said, "Addie, we both need to go into meditation, you know that. We have plenty of time to set up later. Right now we need to prepare ourselves. I will be in my room until you come for me."

Addie nodded in agreement, realizing that Marie must have read her mind. She watched as Marie headed toward the guest room. As soon as she heard the guest room door close, Addie started making calls.

First, she called Tan and asked him to set everything up on that end. The last call she made was to Officer Ed. She asked him if the city would close off access to her lane. She also requested that he talk with the neighbors about it, so they wouldn't be alarmed. He assured her that he would hand pick a couple of men to help. She asked if he planned on being in the house that evening, and If so, she reminded him gently to behave and let Marie do her work. He promised her that he would.

After she hung up, she realized that everything was as ready as it could be.

She moved away from the phone and headed upstairs to her room. She shut the door behind her and pulled the heavy shades down. The room became as dark as the middle of the night. Laying down, she reached over and turned on a small water fountain she had brought back from one of her trips to China. She needed to bring her soul and body into alignment before tonight.

— — — —

"Who was it that called Papa?" Lilly asked, looking at the concerned faces of her father and Mr. Tan, who had stopped talking when she walked into the room.

"You're up sweetheart, we didn't hear you coming," Louis answered, holding his arms open wide, motioning for her to come get a hug.

Tan simply nodded in Lilly's direction. He said, "I'll leave the two of you alone." He walked past Lilly on his way out the door.

Lilly ran over at her father. Scooping her up in his arms, he tried like he always did to hug her tight. Lilly pushed him back, so she could look him straight in the eye.

"We are going to the house, aren't we?" She asked.

"We are if you agree. Addie's friend Marie thinks that Elizabeth wants to talk through you, because you are a little girl just like her. But the important thing is what you want to do."

Lilly asked, "If I let her, will she go away?"

Louis said, "I don't know. She may or she may try to hurt you in some way. That is why the choice is yours, if you want to let her talk through you," he answered, kissing her forehead before letting her go and reaching for her hand.

Lilly let him take her hand and guide her toward the dining room where Tan was setting a place for breakfast. Nick was there, standing near the stove. Tan motioned to the chair pulling it out for her.

Nick said, "Good morning sleepy head. I thought you would never get up. Ready for some of my world famous French toast? I waited to make yours so it would be warm."

"Sir, would you like some more coffee?" Tan asked, walking around the bar into the kitchen.

"Yes please," Louis answered, sitting down at the end of the table with Lilly to his left. Still silent she took a drink of orange juice. Louis was determined to give her all the time she needed without pressing. Tan returned with the coffee, followed by Nick who was holding a plate for Lilly.

Nick had made sure that the plate was perfect. He had placed three pieces of French toast neatly in the center. Each one was dusted with powdered sugar. Two large strawberries cut like a fan were placed on the side. Setting it down in front of Lilly, he smiled at her when she thanked him. He returned to the kitchen and came back with his cup, and sat down on the other side of Lilly.

Louis stirred cream and sugar into his coffee. Just as he brought the cup to his mouth, his daughter spoke.

Lilly said, "She can talk through me, Papa." Then the young girl took a big bite of French toast.

"Are you sure?" Louis asked, setting the cup back down on the table.

"In my dreams, when I first saw Elizabeth, she said she wanted me to be her friend. And friends help friends, right Papa?"

"Well yes, but this isn't like helping a friend with homework. You could get hurt helping this friend," Louis reminded her.

"Like Nick could have gotten hurt when he stopped the boys from hurting me the night they threw rocks at the old house. Or like the way Elizabeth got hurt when she helped her friend?" Lilly asked.

Nick said, "She's got a point. Sometimes, you just gotta do what you gotta do without counting the cost to you."

Louis smiled at the children. He said, "You are both right, and yes friends do help friends."

"Papa, I just thought of something," she said, excitement building in her voice.

"What's that little one?"

"Nick and I will get to stay up late, maybe even all night. If that happens, you wouldn't make us go to school tomorrow, would you? After all, growing children need their sleep."

Louis had to look away to keep from laughing. When he did, he caught Tan looking through the breakfast bar from the kitchen smiling and nodding in agreement with Lilly.

Louis looked at his daughter and said, "You know what I think daughter?"

"What, Papa?" She answered innocently, attempting to wipe up every last drop of syrup on her plate.

"I think you have been spending way too much time with your friend Nick. Then again, he has kept you safe. Not to mention this is the most you have eaten in days. And it has been a long time since I've seen you smile. Tan, I guess the lady of the house has spoken. Let Addie know we are ready whenever they are."

— — — —

Holly had just hung up the phone with Tan. She told him that she would have the dinner meeting catered at Louis's townhouse. From there they could all go to the little brick house, to do whatever it was Marie had in mind.

"I am one lucky girl," Holly told her dog as she gave him the hand signal to remove his huge head from her lap. Getting up from the oversized lounge chair, she dialed the number of the caterer Addie used for private meetings. She knew that Addie would be thrilled with any menu they suggested. Finished with the preparations, Holly headed for the shower.

As Holly walked down the hallway she thought, *mornings like this are what I love most about this job. I hardly ever have to go into the office unless there are clients coming in for meetings or files to close out. Thanks to the boys in the toyshop, I can do all my work from, well anywhere. I am spoiled now. God, I hope this job never ends.*

As she walked through the bedroom on her way to the shower she remembered Addie teasing her about her robe. OK, so she had humored her. She laid the robe across the towel rack next to her towel.

Holly took a long hot shower, using the scented shower gel that Addie had brought back for her from Paris. She had just finished rinsing her hair when she heard her dog, Moe, growl and get up from the bathroom floor. She could hear his nails going across the stone tile floor away from her. He was leaving the bathroom.

Something had to be happening. Moe followed her everywhere. When she was home he never left her side, not even when she was in the bathroom. She was constantly tripping over the oversized Mastiff while she was trying to dry off or put on makeup. She had a strange feeling that they were not alone, and that Moe had taken off to protect her. She decided she was being silly. All of her doors and windows were locked and alarmed.

She dismissed her feeling and finished her shower. Reaching through the curtain for her towel, she couldn't feel it. *It must have fallen off the rack,* she thought as she bent down to feel on the floor outside the tub.

"Looking for this?" She heard Wolff's low voice and felt the towel in her hand. Jumping at the sound of his voice, she lost her balance and felt his arm come through the part in the curtain wrap around her waist steadying her. Then as fast as it happened he removed his arm, never once opening the curtain far enough to see anything. She stood there with a towel in hand.

As Wolff walked out of the bathroom, he called back over his shoulder, "I'll make some coffee. Mac and I will wait for you in the kitchen. Make it fast will you? We have a lot to do before tonight."

She yelled after him, "Keep your orders to yourself Wolff. This is my house and I will be there when I'm good and ready."

Holly couldn't believe Wolff had broken into her apartment, scared her half to death, and now was giving her orders. She was furious with him. She dried her body and opened the curtain just a bit, making sure she was alone. Then she stepped out of the shower and grabbed her robe. Holly combed through her hair and dapped on her most expensive perfume before she left the bathroom. She didn't have to put on make-up. Her cheeks were still pink from her elevated blood pressure.

She knew he had seen the robe in the bathroom, but she'd be damned if he got to see her in it for any length of time. She walked back to her bedroom and grabbed a pair of jeans. She slipped into a sports bra and one of her tight fitting T-Shirts. She'd give him sexy for sure, but not sexy elegant. Not this time.

When she rounded the corner of the hall she saw the two men sitting at the kitchen table. Mac helped himself to a cup of coffee as he read her newspaper. Wolff was doing something with his tablet in one hand, while rubbing Moe's ears with his other. Moe was eating it up, one back paw softly thumping the floor. So much for Moe being a security dog, at least when Wolff was around.

"Is my coffee good?" Holly asked sarcastically.

Mac answered, "Sure is little lady. This is the first time I've had a cup from one of those fancy single cup makers. Good thing Wolff knew how to operate it. I wouldn't have had a clue."

"Well, I would be glad if he learned to knock be..." Before she could get out the rest of her sentence, Wolff was by her side handing her a cup of one of her favorite flavors, hot and steaming. Begrudgingly, she took it from him.

Wolff circled around behind her and stood close enough that she could feel the warmth of his body. Not laying a hand on her, she felt his head bend toward her neck and she could feel his soft quick breath.

Wolff asked, "Is all this for me? If it is, I like it."

She felt her face heat up again and she almost threw the coffee at him when she turned around to face him. "Is what for you, Mr. Wolff."

He smiled, "The coffee. What else do you think I was implying."

Mac let out a couple of coughs and said, "Hey Moe, how about you and I go out here and let these two fight it out?" Mac headed for the living room and Moe followed.

Wolff said, "Did I ever tell you what a good choice in dogs you have sweetheart?"

Holly gritted her teeth. She said, "Don't call me sweetheart. I'm not your sweetheart. You have no right to break into my apartment and scare me half to death. What on earth were you thinking?"

"First, I was thinking I could be your sweetheart. But just as important, Addie sent us over here to talk to you. I know she called you and told you we were coming. Then when we got here, you didn't answer the door. Moe didn't bark either, so I was afraid something bad might have happened. What kind of knight in shining armor would I be if I didn't make sure the princess was safe."

"Are you serious? Do you expect me to believe any of that? I know you, but you don't know me very well. I can take care of myself. And as for being your sweetheart or whatever, what gave you the idea that was ever on my mind?"

"Well honey," he said pulling her close and not letting her wiggle her away. "Let's see, you knew I was coming. You took a shower with something that made you soft to the touch. You picked out a robe that Addie bought you in Paris. I know you just got it out because it showed no sign of being worn recently, there were no wrinkles in it. It was lying on the towel rack, waiting. Last but not least, you took the time to comb your hair and put on the perfume that I know Addie bought for you. She bought that particular scent because it happens to be my favorite. In case you are wondering why I know what Addie brought you back from Paris, It's because I was with her when she bought them for you. As a matter of fact, I picked them out. Should I go on or should I just kiss you. Then we'll both know if this is meant to be." He said, bending down close to her face.

"If you do I will slap your face you arrogant..."

"Fine, have it your way." He said, stepping back from her. "I can wait. None of the women in my life have ever said I rushed through anything." He turned and walked toward the living room while saying, "Can we get to work now? I don't have all day."

Holly stamped her foot a couple of times and took three deep breaths before she followed Wolff into the living room. By the time she did, she was wearing her business face and attitude. She hated that he was so smart and arrogant, but yet she loved it at the same time. And if he wanted a challenge, she was ready to be one.

"Alright Mr. McCoid and Mr. Wolff, what is it that you need me to do," she asked as she crossed the room to her desk. Wolff didn't answer, but continued to sit on the coach, stroking Moe's head on his lap.

Mac blurted out, "Miss Holly is it? I would like it if you would call me Mac, everyone does."

Holly smiled at him. She said, "Mac, please call me Holly. All I know is that Addie wanted me to look up some information for you. What can I help you with?"

Wolff didn't say a word. He just watched her every move. He liked what he saw. Addie was right, once he had taken the time to take a look, he would have to do something about this.

Mac said, "We need to know what we can about the house next to Addie's and the land surrounding it. We would also like to know what was going on in the town during the time of Elizabeth's disappearance. Addie said that you can do magic when it comes to looking up information. Or do you have a crystal ball like Marie?"

Holly laughed, she liked this man. He reminded her of her grandfather. She would enjoy working with him.

"No crystal ball here, but I do have this." She pressed a button and Mac watched as a larger screen came up behind the desk. "This should make it easier for you to follow me." She stood in front of the screen. Using a wireless keyboard to access her computer, she typed in a few characters. With just a few strokes, Holly accessed archives at the local historical society. She sat the keyboard down and walked over to the screen. She started touching the screen with her fingers. They watched as a small icon appeared on the screen.

Mac blurted, "Hey that looks like…"

"One of your finger print pads?" Holly responded.

"Yeah, takes me back to the old days." Mac said as he got up and came to stand beside her for a closer look.

"Well it's not quite the same." Holly said, touching the screen again. "The society's access program recognizes me. It allows me access to information from all over the world. Addie donates a lot of money to the historical society every year, and therefore they have allowed her to, shall we say, use them as a portal. I can access all the courthouse documents in the state and the old newspapers. That will give us a pretty good picture of what was going on back then."

"Won't that take too long?" Mac asked.

"There are several things that I can do to speed it up like using key word searches. I can add up to five at a time. Dates, names or occupations work well too. That is one of the attributes I asked the boys to program in for me. It's not only designed to look for several things at once, but it will also display the information they find in separate windows. That way, I can have a lot of information on one screen at the same time. It also has voice recognition."

They watched as her fingers flew around the screen. Neither Wolff nor Mac had any idea what they were looking at. For a change, Wolff had the feeling he was just along for the ride. When she finally stopped, it was at a map of the river and the surrounding area of the little brick house. There were also several spreadsheets that had popped up behind the picture. They layered themselves on the screen.

Holly said, "This is the time frame Addie wants us to investigate. Let's take a closer look. Here it is, see? Addie's house was not even built yet. In fact, none of them were. The whole block was pasture."

"What is that, right over here down the river?" Mac asked.

"Native American dwellings," Wolff answered.

"So if there was no brick house back then, where did Elizabeth live? Why is she hanging around in that house?" Mac asked.

"Well, let's take a look at the old deeds and see if we can find who owned the land, and when the houses were built. If we can't link Elizabeth to the house, maybe we can link her somewhere else." Holly's fingers were flying across the screen.

"She is fast." Mac said, looking over at Wolff.

Wolff nodded in agreement.

Holly said, "Here we go. It seems that the little house was built sometime after Elizabeth died. Maybe a year or so later, by a man named Meyer. He bought the land from a Mr. Paddington and built the house himself. He lived there until he died, and from that point on it has been passed down through his family. A year or so later, Addie's house was built by a Mr. Armanton. The last few years the little brick house has been rented out to almost anyone they could find. I've seen the house and it's in pretty bad shape."

"Is there a connection between Meyer and Elizabeth?" Wolff asked.

"Let's cross reference articles of the time and their names. Maybe we can come up with more to go on. Wait, here is something on Elizabeth's disappearance. It says that she was the daughter of the mayor. They lived in that big house up on Fourth Street, Wolff you know the one. The whole fence line is planted in red and yellow tulips. That's why Addie plants her flowers in different colors. She thinks that flowers should reflect the same colors as the house."

Mac added, "A Painted Lady, old Victorians like Addie's use to be called Painted Ladies"

"That's right, because of the different colors they used to paint them. That is another reason Addie wanted it," Holly answered. "She loved the name."

"Because it reminds her of New Orleans," Wolff said.

Mac asked again, "So what connection, if any, did Elizabeth have with Meyer?"

Holly answered, "Here it is. He was on the city council and in charge of finances. The paper at that time ran articles about several scandals going on while Elizabeth's father was the mayor. One of them has to do with wood that was supposed to be given to families that couldn't afford it. Many of them were Native Americans." Holly opened another newspaper article on the screen and pointed at it. "It says here that the winter was severe that year. Several people died because they didn't get the wood that was allotted to them. The wood was part of the city's social services. It sounds like our heat assistance today. Look at this, my God they froze to death right in their own homes. The article says that there was an on-going investigation, but the books were all in order."

"You hear that Wolff? Meyer was involved in the finances. My wife's an accountant. She always says that when you have a murder victim, the first things to look at are the books of the people closest to them. Always follow the money first."

Wolff said, "Keep digging Holly. Get back to me as soon as you can. I need to know anything you can find out about the mayor, his wife and any city officials closest to them. I would be willing to bet that one of the three men following Elizabeth was Meyer. Now I want to know who the other two were." He bent down to kiss her cheek from behind before she could move away. When she turned to glare at him, he just smiled back and hurried away.

Before she could throw out a few cuss words at him, he and Mac were out the door. She felt Moe's cold nose poking at her hand. She looked down, pulled her hand back and pointed at his bed. Moe realized he was in the doghouse. He crossed the room and flopped down on his bed looking pathetic.

"Don't even give me that pitiful look," Holly scolded, walking past him to the kitchen to warm her coffee.

# CHAPTER 25

As soon as Addie picked up the phone, and before she could even say hello, Holly started talking.

"Boss, I have found damning information on Elizabeth's evil stepmother and her gang. I think she and the watchers were cooking the town's books. No one noticed because on paper, the books balanced. I'd be willing to bet that there was one that didn't. And besides, no one cared because the only people that it affected were Native Americans. Would you believe the town actually had an energy assistance program back then? But instead of gas, it was wood. It wasn't until some of the town folk died from lack of wood that the citizens demanded an investigation. The Mayor and three of the other city council members were suspect, as well as Elizabeth's stepmother."

Addie asked, "In what way? Just because she was the Mayor's wife?"

Holly said, "No, there was way more to it than that. She owned the town's only general store. Mr. Meyer owned the town's only saloon that was rumored to be a gambling hall and brothel. Mr. Paddington was the army's representative to the Native tribes, who also had a land business. Finally, there was a Mr. Armanton who was a lawyer. Get this, they all new Elizabeth's stepmother from childhood."

"That would make sense. Was she from the area?" Addie asked.

"No, she was from New York. One of the local people that was suspicious was a retired sheriff. He did some digging into her past."

Addie asked, "How do you know that?"

"There was an old diary and some old pictures that one of the decedents donated to the Historical Society. You know that old brick house on the main drag? The one you were thinking about buying?"

"Yes, I know the one," Addie said.

Holly added, "Well back then there was a very beloved old lady that lived in it. She was a kind of grandma to everyone. She fell on hard times and she was one of the people that was supposed to get wood for heating from the city. When she didn't come to church one Sunday, some parishioners went to check on her. Boss, they found her in her rocking chair, frozen stiff. Can you believe that? That poor old lady, it was after finding her body that a few of the town's people took up a collection to hire the old Sheriff to investigate. He found out some things, but nothing that he could use to get them arrested. But he did discover that the group had been involved in business together off and on over the years. They'd never been arrested or convicted, but they had been run out of a town in Pennsylvania for scamming a few of the locals."

"How did they all get out here?" Addie pressed.

"Elizabeth's stepmother, Allina Fitzpatrick, if that was her real name, arrived in town first. She answered an ad for a School Mistress. She was hired and taught for less than a year before she married the owner of the town's general store, a Mr. Olson."

"She knew what she was doing when she latched onto August Olson. August was fifteen years her senior, a widower of four years, and had a three-year old daughter that everyone adored named Elizabeth. They went everywhere together, that is until he met our Allina."

"I can just about imagine that we are talking about the ugly stepmother?" Addie said.

"I'll send you a picture of her. She was a looker. She also wasted no time going after poor August. From what I can tell he was a great guy that everyone loved. He was loved most of all by his little girl Elizabeth and the Native Chief of the area."

Addie said, "That information backs up all of the information we read in both journals, the one from Lilly's family and the one that Wolff found this morning."

Holly added, "August's first wife had been a friend to many of the ladies of the tribe. At her funeral there were more natives that attended than white people."

Addie said, "I take it that was all over when Allina married August?"

"Sure was, she would have nothing to do with the tribe. She was quoted as only referring to them as savages. I can imagine her forbidding August to have anything to do with them, and I bet Elizabeth had to sneak out to see them. One of the Chief's grandson's is named..."

"Two Ponies?" Addie interjected.

"You found verification on that, too? Was it in the book that Wolff found?" Holly asked.

Addie said, "Yes, please go on, sorry to interrupt."

Holly continued, "Addie, one of the reports says that both Two Ponies and Elizabeth went missing the same day. Two Ponies was later found by the river dehydrated. It sounds like he was in shock. Elizabeth was never found. He must have really loved her Addie. After that day, he was known in the tribe as the Brave that wouldn't marry."

Addie asked, "Did Allina bring her other friends to town after she and August married?"

"About a year or so later, right after her husband ran for mayor and won. He turned the store over to her. One of his first orders of business, which I am sure he did with much persuasion, was to inquire from the government about assigning an agent to work with the local tribe. Enter Mr. Paddington. How he finagled himself into that position, who knows."

Addie said, "A good con is a good con, and the government has been full of them since day one. Go on," Addie instructed.

"In a short period of time, the tribe had nothing left. They were being pushed off their land more and more. They were only allowed to communicate through Paddington. Even though their old friend was now the Mayor, they were cut off. In the meantime, Mr. Paddington became very popular among the ladies. As his reputation grew, so did his bank account. There were rumors that he had several affairs with wealthy farmer's wives, and then blackmailed them. He was also appointed to the city council soon after his arrival."

Addie said, "How were you able to find all of this information?"

Holly continued. "Back then, you could write almost anything in the paper. Also, there was the journal that I mentioned was donated by one of the neighbors to the society. I don't think she liked the mayor's new wife at all. The next man on the scene would be our Mr. Meyer, the saloon owner. He came to town with money. He bought the local watering hole and immediately added a second story. He called it a gentleman's club. Of course he had no problems getting permits from the mayor. When a few of the locals complained about what was going on in there, it was hushed up. There are records of several beatings and even one suspicious death that may have been connected."

Addie sighed before saying, "So now we have the town controlled at the mayoral level, the Native American tribe controlled, and a privately owned club to launder money. Perfect. Paddington could carry on his blackmail, Mr. Meyers could make money providing all the amenities to the local gentry, and he may have been involved in blackmail, as well. All we need now is…"

"Enter Mr. Armanton, the lawyer who was also a land agent. With the natives suddenly losing their land, there was more land to buy and sell. Paddington would make deals with the government and the town to obtain the land. Then he would arrange for Armanton and Meyer to buy the land. Of course he charged enormous commissions and fees for setting up all of the deeds and transactions."

"Another way to hide and shuffle money," Addie added.

"Yep, that last step gave them total control of the town. Is it any wonder why they were all appointed to the city council?"

"Not at all, and as time went on they took more and more control for themselves and the town was worse than ever I fear."

"That's right, it lasted for around seven years and then things started to change for them. As the town grew, there were more people and more questions. More residents became involved in the city government and some would not be put off. Plus, the local paper would not let go of the winter deaths that were caused by a lack of fuel that had not been provided. The wood had been paid for by the city, or so the citizens thought."

Addie considered what she had just heard. She said, "So our group of scoundrels had to either find a way to lay low, or cut and run. Did you come across any news about Elizabeth and her father during the time that the scandals were heating up?"

"Not much of anything about Elizabeth, but she was a child. There is news about her father. It seemed he developed a stomach ailment, go figure. He just kept getting sicker and no one could figure out why."

"Right before Election Day, Mr. Armanton stopped by the mayor's office to walk home with him. The paper said that it was their habit to walk together because Armanton only lived a few blocks beyond the Olson house. Anyway, when Armanton reached the mayor's office door, it was standing open. When he went in, he found the mayor crumbled on the floor, dead. He had been struck in the head. The local doctor claimed that he was killed with an axe to the head. He said it had to be a Native American axe. No one questioned him. Can you believe that? But, they didn't arrest anyone and they never found the murder weapon." Holly said.

"I bet they didn't. One loose end was now closed for the scammer. The M.O. of this team is that they leave with no trace. With no past, they also stayed clear of the law. So where does that leave Elizabeth and her stepmother?" Addie said, although it sounded more like she was talking out loud to herself.

Holly said, "Right after the mayor died, Elizabeth disappeared. Do you think they killed her? Not a little girl. They maybe con-artists, but that would make them monsters in my book," Holly said.

Addie said, "I think they were monsters Holly. Remember, we know nothing of their past except for a few cons. You said one report suspected them of beatings and a possible death? And remember the consequences of their stealing firewood to line their own pockets. People died as a result of their greed. To me, that is cold-blooded murder. Knowing how this gang works, they wouldn't kill Elizabeth unless they had no choice, since they could have used her as cover or to make money in some other way."

Holly said, "One part of me needs Elizabeth to tell us what happened to her, but the other part of me is sickened by what we might find out. On a lighter note, the dinner is all set up for tonight. I just hope we don't lose it later."

Addie asked, "Holly, are you having second thoughts about being at the house tonight? If you are, I can get someone else."

Holly answered, "No way, this is my job and if eleven year old kids can be there, so can I. Besides, Mr. T. Wolff will be there to protect me."

Addie grinned and asked, "Are you trying to tell me things went well when he stopped by? Did he like the robe?"

"I didn't wear the robe and when we have some time alone I will tell you all about it."

"You are going to keep me in suspense? That is not fair." Addie said.

Holly responded, "Oh, like not dictating and closing the file on what happened in New Orleans is fair? Both you and Wolff refuse to talk about it. You used more operatives on that one job than any other, not to mention the loss of the senior partners. The file is still not documented."

Addie relented. She said, "Wolff and I were talking about that the other day and you're right. I have to close the file and document what happened. I promise when this is done we will do it together."

"And we'll still call it Pirate's Alley, right?" Holly said before Addie could continue.

"Yes, I promise. I am going to hang up now. I need to meditate for awhile. I will see you at dinner tonight. You did a great job on the research, by the way."

Holly said, "Get it together, Boss. I'll keep digging and see if I can find out more before tonight. I don't know if I should say that I am looking forward to it, but like it or not I'll be there."

# CHAPTER 26

"That was some dinner Addie," Officer Ed said, pushing back his chair. Looking around the table he added, "What's the plan for tonight?"

Setting down her coffee cup, Addie turned to Marie, "The floor is all yours, Marie."

Marie looked around the table at all the expectant faces. Since almost all of them had never experienced communicating with the other side, she wanted to prepare them as much as she could. Then again, just like on this side of the veil, you can never predict for sure how a person will act under a given circumstance. Marie cleared her throat and began.

"First of all, I want to thank you all for the hard work you have done so far and for your willingness to participate tonight, even though many of you don't know what to expect or what to believe."

"Let me start by giving you some background. There are many theories pertaining to multiple layers of time and space. Some say there are as many as ten before you reach what we will call The Light. There are just as many theories as to why someone may choose or have to stay in one layer or another and not go onto The Light when they pass over. Some believe that until we enter into The Light we can go back and forth within the layers. That's why we see some entities, some we only hear, and some we can only feel or smell."

"Let's think of Elizabeth as standing behind a curtain made of silk or gauze. You can see her, but not as clearly as we see each other. From what we have heard her say through Lilly, and what we have read in her journal, we believe that she has unfinished business here that is maybe stopping her from going forward into The Light. Tonight we hope to learn what that business is. We are hoping that once we know, we can help her resolve it. Releasing her to move on and be reunited with her loved ones."

"Before I take any questions, I must tell you that there are certain ground rules I insist on. If there are any of you that would be offended please say so, at which time I will ask you to remain at Addie's house until we are finished."

"You aren't going to make us drink blood or anything like that are you?" Ed asked.

Marie answered, "No Officer, nothing that drastic. What I will ask you to do is be respectful of Elizabeth. She is our guest. It's a privilege to be allowed to communicate with her and it's a privilege to assist her if we can. I will also ask that you not interrupt or try to touch myself, Addie or Lilly, no matter what happens. If at any time we are in meditation or prayer, please do not interrupt. If you have questions for Elizabeth, write them on the sheet of paper that Holly will give you. Holly will give the questions to me and I will ask Elizabeth."

"I'll ask that throughout the process you think of this as a normal discussion with a little girl. Only send feelings her way that you would send any child that you are having a conversation with. One last thing before we go, several of us have read portions of Elizabeth's journal. It appears that several people were involved in ending her life. Let me remind you, they have all passed over. And like Elizabeth, they too could return tonight. If at any time there is a fight to be fought, stay out of it. Again, do not touch myself, Addie or Lilly. Does everyone understand?"

"You mean we can't do anything to help?" Wolff asked.

Marie said, "Thank you for your question, Mr. Wolff. No, not in the way that you are used to. Holly will be providing each of us with an outline of what we plan to do, as well as the words to several prayers that you can say out loud. You must not touch us under any circumstances. Do you understand? I cannot repeat this enough."

Nick said, "I do. Like my mom always tells me, the tongue is mightier than the sword. Did I get that right?"

Marie answered, "Exactly right Nick, and if you want to protect your friend that is the best way to do it."

"Give me a 45 any day," Ed grumbled.

Turning to look at him with sharp clear eyes, Marie answered, " Believe me sir, if this encounter should turn ugly, your 45 will do you no good. If there are no more questions we should get started. I don't want to keep Elizabeth waiting. Nick, do you have the list of things I asked you to bring?"

"Yes ma'am. White candles, sage, paper, pencils, and small flashlights. I have them all in my backpack ready to go," Nick answered.

"Thank you Nick. Mr. Wolff?"

"The house is ready. Table, chairs, cameras and sound equipment, just like you instructed. We have the two technicians you requested from Addie's crew standing by in their van outside, but I do have one question."

"Yes."

"Should I be prepared to handle a similar situation as New Orleans?" Wolff asked.

Marie smiled, "Mr. Wolff, that encounter was an extremely rare one. I don't believe that there are entities like those we encountered in the City of the Dead present in this area. Certain areas, because of what happened in their the past, draw certain types of entities. New Orleans is one of those cities. However, as I have already said, we need to be prepared for anything. This time you will be on your guard, and I have every faith in you Mr. Wolff. Now, if there are no more questions, we should go." They stood to leave, each one filing out of the townhouse to their vehicles. Wolff and Mac waited for Marie to pass by them. As she did, she smiled knowingly at Wolff. He offered her his arm to walk her to the car that he would be driving.

Wolff leaned over and said, "Marie, I want you to know, this time I am ready for them and whatever they try to throw at us. You believe that, don't you?"

"I do Mr. Wolff, I do."

# CHAPTER 27

Inside the little house Marie directed everyone to their places. As the outline instructed, Marie led them all in a prayer of protection and welcome. They were asked to sit and watched as Marie, assisted by Nick, lit the candles and seated Lilly in a rocking chair and placed her feet on a footstool. Marie placed a tray on Lilly's lap, on which Nick laid a drawing pad and pencil. He then took a chair next to Lilly's rocker.

Marie asked Wolff to turn off all the lights. From that point on, everyone saw a side of Marie that was very different from the soft-spoken, shy woman that they knew. Marie was in complete control. She appeared to be stronger than ever and spoke in a firm, clear voice. They watched as she lit a single white candle and the small torch made of sage, and walked around the room stopping at all four corners to recite a blessing on the room and all that were present. Returning to the table, she gave thanks. Once she was done she stopped, closed her eyes and waited.

As they watched, her face went very calm and her breathing slowed. She looked like she was asleep. She said nothing. All was quiet, but not all was calm as they would later see from the video of the evening. Wolff, Mac and Louis seated along the back wall of the room were the first to register change on their faces. Wolff would later describe it as a cold that made him shudder. It was so intense that it seemed to go not around him, but through him, chilling him all the way to the bone. Mac felt it too. One by one, it seemed to make its way through everyone. It was like watching a wave as they all shuddered one after another, even officer Ed.

Behind the cold came the smell. Gone was the leafy sent of the sage Marie had used to cleanse the room, replacing it was an overly sweet smell of flowers. Looking at each other they could tell that everyone smelled the same fragrance.

When they looked back to Marie, they noticed that she was smiling.

Marie opened her eyes and looked in Lilly's direction. There, next to Lilly's chair was a faint blue light. They watched as the light moved closer to Lilly. Louis seated between Wolff and Mac, tensed as the light drew closer to Lilly. Seeing Louis's agitation, they each laid a hand on Louis, just in case.

Looking over at her father as if she felt his tension, Lilly said, "It's alright Papa, she won't hurt me."

Wolff and Mac felt Louis's body relax under their grip. They removed their hands, but remained on guard.

"Elizabeth," Marie said, "We are all here to help you. We found your book. You are a very bright young lady. Lilly regards you as a friend and is willing to allow you to use her body to speak to us. Please consider her feelings always and show her the same consideration that she is showing you. Nick is a neighbor and friend to Lilly, just as you and Two Ponies were friends. Nick wants to help. He has provided you with writing materials if you would feel more comfortable communicating with us in that way."

As they watched, the blue light moved from the side of the chair to between Lilly's legs, then it dissolved backwards just as Lilly had when she sat down in the chair. Lilly shuddered slightly, then looked straight ahead through eyes that were not hers. Elizabeth was back and by the look on her face, she was uncomfortable with the confinements of this body and the clothes that Lilly was wearing. For a minute or two she kept looking at her bare legs under the shorts that Lilly was wearing. She looked at her legs then looked at everyone. Once she realized that no one seemed to find the apparel offensive, she relaxed.

Marie simply waited, and Elizabeth spent a few more seconds looking around the room, searching the faces as if she were making sure of something. It was as if she were trying to recognize someone or trying to decide if it was safe to talk. Then, with what seemed like a great effort for her at first, she spoke through Lilly.

"The men who watched me said that they wanted to help."

Marie answered, "I know Elizabeth. I know they lied to you. I know they hurt you. We want to help you. The choice is yours."

As they watched, Lilly started to rock the chair back and forth, moving her head from side to side. She then spoke again in the singsong voice they had heard before.

*"Help me, help me, help me if you can,*
*Find me, find me if you can,*
*The hole where I am is dark and wet,*
*And the rock is black and heavy."*

As they listened, Lilly's voice seemed to rise. She became angry and her body tensed as she gripped the arms of the rocker.

*"I was broken, I was bleeding,*
*They thought I was dead, but I was breathing,*
*They wanted to win the praise of many,*
*For hanging a man whose only crime was his family,*
*It was not his time, it was not my time,*
*I would not tell them, so they broke my bones,*
*They bound me up to hide the truth,*
*But no matter how heavy or black the rock may be,*
*free one day my bones will be"*

The room was quiet as each person tried to make sense of the poem. The silence was broken when Marie continued her questions.

"Elizabeth, we know that you are angry, but your anger is holding you here. What can we do to help you forgive, so you can move on?" Marie asked, she had barley gotten the words out when Elizabeth screamed through Lilly.

"Find me, untie me, and let me breathe,
Take my bones to those I trust,
Let them bury me."

"With your help Elizabeth we can do that," Marie said, "My friend Addie is trying to locate where your father and mother are buried, so we can reunite you with them."

Suddenly, the room grew frigid and the sweet smell was replaced by a rotting stench. The smell was so strong that gagging could be heard around the room. Holly opened windows, trying to let in some fresh air. She had just returned to her seat when there was a loud banging sound and all of the windows slammed back down.

Almost instantly, they watched a gray mist form in front of Lilly's chair. Wolff and Mac grabbed for Louis and held him tight. Marie and Addie stood to face the mist, as Holly started to recite a prayer. The others began searching their papers to find the prayer, and then joined in. Sweeping the tray from her lap, Lilly stood to face the mist too.

"Tell them stepmother, you evil witch, tell them all. Tell them why you cursed a family and how you died. Tell them why I am still here!" Elizabeth shouted.

As they watched, the mist struck out hitting Lilly, causing her to fall back into the chair.

"Stop," Marie said firmly "You are bound by heaven from touching this child. If you want to speak, speak through me."

The mist seemed to be gathering itself as it moved closer to Marie, and then dissolved into her. Marie's body straightened stiffly and anger changed her features. Louis struggled to free himself, but Wolff and Mac held him tight. Marie turned to Elizabeth, but made no move toward her. Addie moved closer to Marie and was reciting a verse of some kind that Wolff recognized as Hebrew. This one was not on anyone's papers. It was like Marie could talk but not move. When Addie saw that the she was controlled, Addie stepped forward to address her.

"Ma'am, you were not invited to this house. I demand by heaven that you tell us who you are and why you are here."

"I don't need your invitation," The woman spat at Addie, "This is my stepdaughter, my property if you will, and I will deal with her anyway that I see fit," She answered, trying to point at Elizabeth.

"You will do as we allow," Addie answered, "She is with us and protected by us. I repeat, why are you here? Speak your peace before I banish you."

"I am here to keep this child from telling her lies. She is a stupid, evil child. I wanted no part of her then, and I want no part of her now."

Elizabeth screamed, "You are the liar! You are the one who told them to watch me. You are the one who gave me hot milk to drink which made me still, and then took me to them!"

"Lies, all lies!" The woman screeched back.

"No, truth! You stood by and watched while they asked me over and over again about the Chief and Two Ponies. When I wouldn't tell, they tied my mouth and hit me over and over again. They broke me." Elizabeth shrieked. "They hit me one time too hard and I fell and hit my head on the rock."

"When I woke up, I saw my body wrapped up in rags and tied tight with twine. I couldn't scream, I couldn't move, but I could see. They thought I was dead when they put me in that dark, wet hole, but you knew I wasn't dead. You told them you needed to say goodbye, so you came and stood over the hole. You had the lantern in your hand, and you saw my eyes were open. You saw my eyes…"

"You pulled back the light and told them to cover the hole with that big black rock. It was too dark for them to see my eyes because you had the light. You killed me. It was not my time. Then you told everyone that I had disappeared, and that the natives had done something to me. But Mr. Meyer was going to tell, wasn't he mama? He couldn't live with what he had done. He was going to tell and you knew you would hang, just like my friend. So you all made a plan to make it look like you ran to the river and drowned. If the town thought you were dead, you could take the money and run."

"But it wasn't the end that you thought it would be was it? Because the river was too strong that year, and I was there. You saw me. I called to you about the rocks in your dress hem, remember? You had been so vain about how your dress hung when you walked that you had sewn small rocks all around the hem of your dress. You died with a curse on your lips. I sat on the beach watching the water take you down and I laughed. Two Ponies saw you die too. Two Ponies had been watching when you killed me, so he didn't try to help you. He sat with me on the beach and watched as the river took you down."

"You thought that you had only hurt one family, but you have been tied here too. You are tied to their family, tied to killing over and over again, but you are dead like me."

The stepmother yelled, "You think you know you are a stupid child! You thought you could disobey me then and I showed you. Just like you think you can save them now, but I will show you."

"You are right Madame, she can't stop you, but I can." Louis said.

Marie whirled to face him, glaring at him. The look on her face was daring him to try.

The stepmother spat out, "You, stop me? You are not even half a man. Your ancestor tried to stop me and I watched him hang. The rest of your pitiful family has tried to stop me, but I have taken one after another to their graves. I am already dead little man, how will you stop me?"

"I can, on behalf of my ancestors, forgive you. You no longer have any power over our family because I forgive you." Louis answered.

Marie screamed curses at him, as Addie stepped forward demanding the woman leave her body and be gone. As they watched, a murky gray mist came out of Marie. Marie fell back into Martin's arms. Holly wiped Marie's face as Martin prayed over her. The mist seemed to swirl around Addie like it was trying to enter her, but couldn't. Standing her ground, Addie addressed the ugly mass.

"Madame, you have no more hold over anyone in this room now that the truth is known and forgiveness has been given. You will go to your place and be judged by he who has that right. We will find your innocent daughter and set her free. We will right the wrong that you did, and Elizabeth will feel the light on her face again."

Again, the smell seemed to overpower the room as the windows opened and shut so violently that every pane of glass was broken. The candle blew out, and Nick's backpack flew across the room just missing Addie's head. She stepped aside, but held her ground.

"I call forth the power of heaven through the blood of Jesus Christ to bind you now until the day you meet your judge from walking the earth. Be bound and be gone now." Addie demanded.

Then, the scream of someone being tortured filled the little house, as violently as it came, the mist seemed to melt into the floor. As it did Once again the room was warm, quiet and filled with an overly sweet scent of flowers.

Addie rushed over to Lilly who was leaning against Nick, holding his hand. She was tired, but unharmed. Addie felt a hand on her shoulder and turned to see Louis standing there waiting to take his daughter. Moving aside to let him comfort her, Addie kept telling her that it was over. Nick moved over next to Addie, his mother at his side stroking his hair and telling him over and over how much she loved him.

Looking up at Addie, he saw Martin with his arm around Addie's shoulders, while Holly handed Marie a glass with a small amount of dark brown liquid in it. Wolff, Mac and officer Ed were no longer in the house.

"Addie," Nick said, pulling on her shirtsleeve.

"What is it Nick?" Addie asked.

"I think I know where she is."

"Where who is? Nick."

"Elizabeth, I think I know where Elizabeth is." Nick answered, pulling away from his mother heading for the door.

"Addie don't let him go alone. Follow him while I get some tools." Martin said.

"Right," Addie said, leaving them and running after Nick, letting the door slam behind her. Calling back to the other men and technicians to bring the cameras and follow them, she ran after Nick, his mother close behind.

They saw him heading for the steps behind the gazebo. He called for them to hurry.

"Wait for me Nick. I don't want you falling down those steps." Addie called after him. As she passed the gazebo, she flicked the switch turning on the white icicle lights that Martin left up all year long. They provided just enough light for the group to make it down the steps safely.

Martin and the crew were close behind. Not knowing exactly what would be needed, Martin handed Wolff some tools and rope from the back of his truck. Then he had gone back to the garage, and with help from the technicians, had positioned a set of his high-powered work lights on the bank pointing over the edge. When he flipped the switch the whole area below lit up.

By the time he got to the bottom of the stairs, Wolff and Mac had the rock tied up and were ready to try and move it. Mac stood aside and let Martin take his place while he grabbed for his camera. He was going to get pictures of this.

From the bank above they heard, "Hey Martin, need a hand down there? You young people are going to have to keep it down, it's late." Looking up they saw the neighbors lining the bank. Officer Ed was instructing his men to hold them back while trying to explain crime scene procedure.

# CHAPTER 28

When the rock was moved, they found Elizabeth's remains. She looked like a small mummy, being wrapped the way she was. Lilly cried. Marie, watching from above in the gazebo, hung her head to whisper a prayer. Mac wiped at his eyes and started taking pictures. Officer Ed made a call to the County Medical Examiner's office telling them to send only Dr. Lindsey. He didn't want anyone else on this crime scene.

A few days later, Dr. Lindsey and the state archeologist called a press conference. They explained that the body of a child dating back to around the time of the civil war had been found on state property. The Tribal Council had claimed the body, and agreed to perform burial rights and bury her on reservation property. It was a private ceremony.

It was a beautiful day when Elizabeth was laid next to the family of her dear friend. Over her grave, Addie and Marie planted a wild flower that Elizabeth had identified in her book as being one of her favorites, along with a single lily of the valley in honor of her newest friend. When an article regarding the police finding Elizabeth's body had finally been released in the local newspaper, a man came forward claiming to be a descendant of the Meyer family. He had met privately with Addie and Wolff at the office. He confirmed that his great-grandfather had confessed to the events of that horrible night, and described the part that he had played in Elizabeth's death.

He verified that Elizabeth's stepmother had been involved with the three men that Holly had identified. His great-grandfather was one of the three men. It seemed that they had also used the uprising that was going on around that time as part of their cover.

What Holly hadn't found was that Two Ponies had hidden a set of books that would have hung them all. They needed to discredit the Chief before he exposed them. That is why they were watching Elizabeth and trying to learn the Chief's whereabouts. Later, they found out that Elizabeth didn't know that the Chief had escaped to Canada, and the Chief didn't know that Two Ponies had hidden the books that would have implicated them.

When they found out that the chief had left some kind of written account with his wife, the plan was for Elizabeth's stepmother to cause a diversion at the hanging. By faking a suicide attempt, while the townspeople were distracted by the hanging and trying to stop Elizabeth's stepmother, the three men were supposed to grab the Chief's wife and get the book from her.

But just like the original plan, things went horribly wrong. When Elizabeth's stepmother cursed the Chief's wife, she went into labor and there were too many people around her for the men to be able to grab her. When Elizabeth's stepmother jumped into the river, it was stronger than she had expected. When they found her body, they found the small rocks that she had used as weights, which were sewn into the hem of her dress. They were used to make the dress hang properly when she walked, but they acted as weights to pull her down into the river. Instead of getting away to meet up with her partners later, she drowned.

As the story went after the hanging, Mr. Armanton petitioned the court and confiscated the belongings of the Chiefs wife, which included the book. Once he determined that there was no damaging information about him, Mr. Paddington decided to stay on.

Mr. Paddington was promoted for bringing the Chief to justice and returned back east. Mr. Meyers sold the saloon and gave away most of his money to charities. He bought the land and built the little brick house, which he lived in until he died. Mr. Armanton bought the land next door and built the huge Victorian that Addie now lives in, to make sure that

Mr. Meyer didn't do anything stupid.

"He told my grandfather what was done was done, and he just wanted to make sure that no one ever found the body. On his deathbed, he told my grandfather that he had been haunted by Elizabeth ever since that night. She would come to him and beg him to tell the truth and set her free."

"We all thought it was the ramblings of a senile old man. We had no idea that it could actually be a true story." He told Addie. On behalf of his great-grandfather, he wanted to pay for a memorial stone for Elizabeth. Addie made the arrangements. The stone was beautiful and read:

> *To our Elizabeth*
> *There is no greater Love than that of a friend*
> *Who lays down their life for a friend.*

Addie had promised not to reveal his confession or involvement, just as she had kept Marie's involvement from the press.

— — — —

"Well wife, I have to admit that it sure is nice to have our house and gazebo back to normal," Martin said, rocking his chair back and forth.

"You can say that again. Are you still glad you married me?" Addie asked.

"You know it." Martin smiled, stopping to lean over and kiss her.

"Gross, is that all you guys ever do?" Nick said, almost falling into the door as he threw his bike down and came in. "Look what I've got."

"What's that," Martin asked, giving Addie one last kiss just to spite Nick.

"The official story from the *Sun Times* and you know they can't be wrong." Nick said sarcastically, "Like I ever believe anything they print."

"So what did they say?" Martin asked.

"The official story is that Mr. Louis Brisbaux from Canada discovered the body of a young girl, while working for the city planners office. It sseems that he had been on the site where the body was found, directing some of his workmen in removal of what they thought was just another large rock blocking easy access to the sewer drains. When they moved the rock, they found her and called the police. The rest is history, as they say. Some pile of crap isn't it." Nick added, grabbing a cookie from the plate as he turned and headed for the door.

"Young man, do you eat with that mouth?" Martin asked, "Where are you off to in such a hurry?"

"Where do you think? I got a date, or should I say a double date?" Nick answered.

"A double date?" Addie asked.

"Yeah. Lilly, me, my mom and Louis." He called back over his shoulder as he rode off toward home.

Addie and Martin turned and looked at each other.

"Are you thinking what I'm thinking wife?" Martin asked.

"Maybe, that is if you are thinking what happens if Nick's mom marries Louis and Nick and Lilly end up together someday? That could be weird."

"Yeah, that sounds like one of your country songs to me." He said laughing.

"Remember husband, knocking country music to a big time fan who carries a gun is not a good idea."

Standing, Martin walked over to her chair and pulled her up into his arms. He bent down and kissed her on her pouting mouth. He lifted his head and said, "Wife, I'm more worried about you not giving me any more kisses than I am about you shooting me."

# DEDICATION

Thank you God, for the small piece of magic found in every story.

To Randy, the greatest husband in the world, always there with his love and support.

To my sons and grandchildren they are the joy of my life. If it weren't for them my soul would be empty.

To Mom and Dad who always encouraged me to do whatever I wanted and never, ever give up.

A special thanks to my mentor and friend not to mention one of my favorite authors Pat Dennis.

A special thanks to my editors, Cindy Leete and Laura Johnson, who know the fine art that is grammar. I am forever grateful for all their guidance.

To the friends and authors who helped me view storytelling in a whole new light. Marilyn Victor, Gary Bush, and Chris Everheart. I was privileged to share a writing table with them for a while as well as their friendship.

Thank you Christian Kane, for the music I listen to when I write.

# ABOUT THE AUTHOR

L. W. Edwards enjoys a career in Medical Devices where she has been privileged to come in contact with some of Americans finest servicemen. Her curiosity of the paranormal has introduced her to those who enjoy the supernatural as much as she does. She lives along the Minnesota River with her husband enjoying her gardens and as many books as her house can hold. To her there is no end to the adventure here or hereafter.

*Author Photo by Jennifer M. Tjernagel - Studio 241 Photography*